THE WITCHES' OWN

BY

EVELYN KLEBERT

The Witches' Own
By Evelyn Klebert

A Cornerstone Book
Published by Cornerstone Book Publishers

First Cornerstone Edition - 2012
Second Cornerstone Edition – 2021
Third Cornerstone Edition - 2024

Cornerstone Book Publishers
Hot Springs Village, AR
www.cornerstonepublishers.com

ISBN: 978-1613420584

Dedication

For All Those Seeking Their Path
And All Lightworkers in the World Who Toil to Make a
Difference

Table of Contents

THE WITCHES' OWN

THE WRITER

Chapter 1

A town has a texture, a character, a tapestry woven through it, invisible yet as tangible as a bright red stripe painted right down the middle of Main Street. It breathes like a living entity, whether acknowledged or not. And here in Kilmarnock, I would have to observe that most of the time, it went unacknowledged, as did those pesky things that small-town citizens preferred didn't exist.

"What are you doing?"

I looked up from my laptop into the clear, crystal blue eyes of the one shining spot I'd found since I'd moved to this coastal Virginia region nearly a month ago. I smiled broadly at the lovely vision that was also the editor and chief of *The Rappahannock Report.* "You don't want to know," I answered, softly closing the lid on my work.

The lady, one Annie Davenport, was a long-legged blond with a dazzling smile and no-nonsense attitude that I found refreshing and, yes, at times, a bit intoxicating. She sat down next to me at the picnic table that I'd opted to settle at for a time. There weren't a great many parks in this largely rural area, but I had managed to find one niche right along the water that I often escaped to. "You're not bashing our lovely little town, are you Mr. worldly writer from the big city?" she teased, but with the slightest edge in her voice that only one adept at dealing with subtlety might pick up. After all, whatever I might think, it was clear to me that Annie Davenport loved this town and was protective of it.

I smiled at her dancing blue eyes and wondered again why I hadn't asked her out. Oh yeah, I was avoiding involvements here, just looking to write my book for the six months while I ensconced myself in the little town. "Why would you think that, Annie?" I asked, feigning innocence, albeit not too convincingly.

"Just a vibe," she murmured.

I smiled. It was difficult for me not to smile when she was around. I guess it was a crush, a little embarrassing to admit at my age. But if truth be told, it was eerie how many things she'd called correctly over our short acquaintance. I wasn't at all sure if it was feminine intuition or some strange psychic awareness. "Interesting vibe?"

"So, you didn't answer me."

"Oh, just working on my book. That's what I do, and yes, I guess you could say I was bashing the town."

She frowned, staring out toward the small stretch of beach, and I mean small. "You really don't like it here."

I shrugged. That was a good question. Did I really not like it here? "I don't know. It has a lot of atmosphere, is definitely picturesque."

She smiled again, and I really liked it when she smiled. "That's very non-committal, Mr. McQuade."

"Well, if it were a perfect spot, it wouldn't be very conducive to a horror novel, would it? And don't forget. I bring a bad attitude that colors everything I touch."

"You know, if you give it time, this place might just wipe away some of that. It helped —"

Then she stopped. Candid as she appeared at times, Annie Davenport wasn't really one for self-confessions. She was too practical. What I'd gleaned during our very short acquaintance was that the lady in question was around her early thirties, the victim of divorce, as was I, and I didn't use that word victim lightly. She apparently had transplanted back to this area two years ago to keep an eye on her ailing aunt, who lived in a local nursing home. Let's see, and she worked as editor of the local rag and moonlighted as an English teacher at the town's community college. "Well, if it helped you, I think that's great. Me, on the other hand, well, I'm a hard case."

"Yeah," she laughed, something else I liked about her, her soft, infectious laugh, "so I've observed."

"You didn't tell me what brought you here."

"Oh, just a whim. I'm on my way back from class, and I felt a pull here." More of that untapped psychic stuff from her.

There was definitely something different about her — something that pulled me like a magnet, whereas most other people kind of left me untouched. But then again, I'm the guy avoiding involvement. "Never ignore those whims, Ms. Davenport. You have no idea where they might lead."

She smiled again. "Are you going to the antique festival this weekend?"

"Is there such a beast?"

"You really don't read the local paper, do you?"

"With all due respect to your talents, I do avoid it."

"Well, if you find yourself at loose ends, Mr. McQuade, give me a call." She dropped a small business card down on the jagged surface of the well-worn picnic table. "I might be able to introduce you to a bit of civilization around here." Then she stood up, "Or rather what we call Kilmarnock-style civilization."

I picked up the card. In a flourish written across the front was *Rappahannock Report*, Editor, and Chief Annie Davenport. "Although your description tends to chill my blood, I may take you up on it."

She laughed, walking away. "Jump in the water, Peter."

I watched her walk up to her fire engine red SUV and climb in. *Jump in the water*— what a concept.

Who am I?

Is this one of those deep philosophical existentialist-type inquiries? Or am I just full of bullshit? No, don't answer that.

Yes, I'm a writer, making a living writing horror-type novels. I say type because it's never good to box oneself in. I've done horror, espionage, adventure, gothic, mildly romantic paranormal, novelizations of movies, same for TV shows, had my name on a few screenplays. Often enough, whatever pays the bills.

Do I sound jaded?

Sorry, I'm fresh off of a divorce, actually not so fresh, coming up on three years this July. I guess actually divorced for two, but the separation, physical one, has been three years, and the spiritual one, well, that one you could call five or more. My kids might say more.

I have two, a boy and a girl — the older boy, Chris, in college, the girl Jessie, headed that way next year. And their mother engaged to remarry someone "more stable." And you wonder why I don't want to get involved again. Oh, don't get me wrong. There have been women. I like the company of women, just not for too long. Does that make me an SOB? Lily might think so. But my kids, God Bless them, still love me, and even Jessie tells me, "I like you better now, Dad. You're not trying to be something you're not." So, I'm forty-five and now able to do crazy things like falling off the face of the earth, renting a riverside cottage in remote, nowhere Kilmarnock, VA, to write a book which I should probably be doing now, instead of involving myself in all this journal, self-indulgent crap.

I was to meet her there, somewhere amid mingling townsfolk. It was a sunny day in April. The temperature was still indecisive, caught somewhere between the end of winter and the beginning of spring. Back home, which was the grand old city of New Orleans, it would be already slipping into pre-summer. Spring never really happened down there — nothing temperate, nothing lukewarm, just extremes. That was part of the reason for this six-month exodus. I needed to pull myself out of my rut, completely yank myself from what was familiar and plunge into an alien landscape. And I had to admit, just walking the stony streets of Kilmarnock did feel alien, as though I had nothing in common with its residents. I wasn't sure yet if this was the kind of stimulation conducive to a writer's imagination. The jury was out, way out. Thus, far outside of scribbling notes and impressions and doing an almost daily introspection in my journal, not much writing was going on, although I had planned the first month as relaxation and absorption. That was the plan, but not producing was making me antsy.

I meandered down the street. There were pockets of exhibitions on various lawns, and lawns in Kilmarnock weren't small like back home. Potentially they could spread out into acres, but these seemed to keep confined into the range of half an acre a piece, roughly. Some were extensive with antiques, and some sparse. There were booths here and there, some with food, some with other smaller items. All in all, it felt controlled, sedate, nothing like the festivals around the French quarter or uptown. But then again, this was what I wanted — different.

As I continued to walk, I remembered where it was, not far down the road, that old museum, Kilmarnock Historical something or other. I could see it already. Some furniture set up on its long greenish-gray lawn, chairs, tables, a hutch or two. The building itself was a faded red brick, and outside it was trees. There was an expanse of towering trees but one in particular that seemed to stretch straight up to the sky but also had several strong limbs perpendicularly jutting out — a maple or perhaps an oak. Sadly, to say, my knowledge of foliage was remarkably deficient. I stopped beneath it, looking skyward at its trunk that theoretically, or at least in my imagination, seemed to pierce the clouds. Beside me, also oddly and out of place, was a tall, straight-back chair that looked suspiciously to be cherry wood, clearly part of the antique festival.

Undaunted by my surroundings, my eyes felt compelled to follow the lines of the tree upward, and I felt a stirring. It was quite old. This I could feel in my bones — one of those ancient monuments on the earth outside of and yet marking time.

"Do you like the chair?"

It was startling. In my odd musing, I had surely felt alone, completely forgetting that there was still a world milling about. "Oh yes, it seems nice."

The short, gray-haired woman beside me smiled broadly, "It's a steal at two hundred."

"Two hundred dollars?" I suppose I should have tried, but I couldn't disguise my astonishment.

She frowned, a bit of the cheerfulness dissipating from her cherubic face. "It is an antique."

"Yes, and I suppose that puts it out of my budget."

Her mouth quirked a bit in a semi-smile. "Well, that's fair and honest." And then she eyed me with further curiosity. "You're that writer fellow from way down South."

"Um," I held out his hand, feeling at a distinct disadvantage, but that was nothing new. "Peter McQuade." She squeezed my hand with her own, a firmer grip than one might expect from such a tiny person.

"Flora Catlett. I'm related to your landlady. Bess is my cousin. She mentioned you, but the name went by me."

Cousin? That's right. I had tripped across an abnormally high degree of cousins in this little town. "I was just admiring this tree. It seems, well, very old." I realized after I spoke what an odd comment this sounded like. But Flora Catlett seemed completely unfazed.

"Several hundred years, that one. Captured your writer's imagination, I suppose."

I laughed at her directness. "Yes, there is something about it."

She nodded. "Well, of course, it was probably a hanging tree back in the day. This little plot of land used to be a sort of town square at one time. Those stocks in front of the museum aren't just for show. They're originals," she informed me in her soft Virginia drawl.

"Who did they hang here?" I murmured.

Her eyes narrowed a bit. "All kinds I understand, thieves, murderers, witches."

I looked at her a bit blankly. "You're kidding, witches?"

She shrugged, "There was a rich Puritanical tradition around here, amongst other things. I'm sure more than one woman found herself under the gun in the old days."

"Barbaric," I muttered under my breath.

She smiled oddly, as though she wasn't in total agreement. "I suppose so."

I looked closer with a prickling curiosity. You never really knew what was under a stone until you turned it over. "Not a fan of those accused of witchery Flora Catlett?"

After staring pensively at the old tree, she turned back to me, smiling. She shook her head as though to brush some deeper consideration away. "I don't know, Mr. McQuade. I try not to take too firm a judgment on things I don't understand. Plenty of old records are in the museum if you're interested in history. I've organized and preserved quite a number of them myself. You see, I'm a bit of a history buff myself. But what seemed clear was that it was strange times long ago. Not at all like now, so it's hard just to stamp our modern judgment on something we can't understand."

I nodded, soaking in her comments, unexpected wisdom from an unexpected source. "Hmm, sounds intriguing, Flora. I'm not ashamed to say I'm looking for something to ignite my imagination. What exactly would I have to do to get a look at some of those old records?"

She eyed me with sharp, narrowed eyes. "Know the right person." She reached into her skirt pocket and handed me a card for the museum. "I'm here at the museum on Tuesdays and Thursdays. Give me a call once this craziness is over. We'll see what we can set up."

And just then, I noted Annie Davenport crossing the great lawn with her long shapely legs. She was dressed in a white cap, navy shirt, and white shorts, the epitome of spring. "Flora, hi. I see you've met our reclusive writer."

Flora responded with a deep cackle sort of laugh. "Yes, already he's trying to get some of the town's dark secrets out of me."

Annie smiled broadly, "Glad to see you here, Peter. Somehow, I had a feeling you might not show."

"Well, I hope I'm not that undependable."

Flora patted me smartly on the shoulder just to let me know, I thought perhaps, that I'd passed some initial scrutiny. "I'm off to mingle. Take care of him, Annie."

She watched Flora walk away, then looked at me with interest. "What in the world were you two talking about?"

I shrugged a bit, "Witches."

LUCY BONNER

Chapter 2

"How's the book coming?"

"Why do you stay here?" I asked her distractedly. We were eating soft serve ice cream and meandering down Main Street, past one collection after another of antiques that both of us had ceased to acknowledge some time ago.

She laughed, "That's an odd question, Peter McQuade. It's my home. My aunt is in a nursing home here, and I feel connected to the place."

I shook my head, "Sorry, I guess that seems kind of rude. You just seem like you don't fit here."

Annie continued walking slowly, staring off as though absorbing all that was around her. "That's quite an assumption from our short acquaintance Mr. McQuade." She did that from time to time, reverted to Mr. McQuade when she wanted to put distance between us. I wasn't a fool or in any way imperceptive, but this little flirtation, if you will, suited Annie Davenport as well as it suited me. Fun, not complicated, not dangerous, and we could both pretend quite expertly that it was nothing. But the problem was that I was growing tired of living with nothing.

My ice cream was melting right over the sides of the cone, and I was growing tired of that too. I plunked it irreverently into a trash can on the side of the road we passed. "Why aren't you dating anyone?" I asked, still digging.

She laughed, tossing her head a bit. "No time, between the paper and teaching, there isn't much left. Besides, I'm not good at that kind of stuff."

"Clarify," I prodded.

"You are in an odd mood today. It must have been all that talk of witches with Flora Catlett."

"That was research. This is personal."

"Hmm, well, I don't want to end up in one of your books."

"Are you just going to dodge everything today, Annie?"

She sighed, pausing on the edge of a small park in front of the post office. "What are you looking for, Peter?" she asked, smiling at me with little emotion.

"Trying to get to know you better."

"Why is that?"

I shook my head a bit. Good question. I didn't know exactly what I wanted, just that I wanted. "You're a puzzle and an enigma, and I like you."

She turned her clear blue eyes on me speculatively. "Um, let's see. I'm not good at relationships. My marriage was a disaster. He made a fool out of me running around behind my back with other women, destroyed my confidence. So, I usually don't bother with that."

"Some people simply aren't right for each other."

"No kidding," she murmured. "Want to sit down for a moment? I'm getting tired."

There was a stone bench to the left of the small post office that we settled on. "I'm sorry I pushed."

"No, you're not," she said, licking the ice cream cone she was still holding. "It's your nature to ferret out answers."

I shook my head and looked up into the nearly flawless blue sky. You didn't see skies like this back home. Not so pure. "You think you understand me."

"No, I wouldn't go that far. So, tell me about your book. I want to think about something other than my life now."

So, I told her about the tree, Flora Catlett's hanging tree that pierced the clouds.

The dreams began to come. That was how I wrote, mostly from the seeds that were planted in dreams. My daughter Jessie believed that it was a gift sent to me. I didn't not believe nor truly accept. I simply waited and watched.

But I'd known as soon as I'd laid eyes on it that the tree was the spark.

I was a spectator in this one, simply watching. She was beautiful, but of course, she was, dressed in a long white cotton shift. But her black hair was wet, streaming over her pale skin.

Two men had dragged her from a wagon, and the townspeople gathered around as though for a show. "Lucy Bonner," the name was spoken by a tall man garbed in a black robe. "You have undergone the trials at the river banks and have failed. You are condemned to death for the crimes of demonic sorcery. Do you have anything to say?"

She was on her knees, hands tied behind her back, but shakily she came to her feet. With a quick sharp fling, she tossed her hair behind her shoulders. I moved closer, closer, although I felt somehow that I wasn't really there at all. "I am innocent," she spoke in a clear, strong voice, too clear for someone who had endured so much.

My eyes snapped open. I was on the small sofa in the den of Bess Greenlief's cottage. The clock on the wall read 3:00 PM. This morning's meeting at the Kilmarnock Museum had left an imprint. I sat up, slowly trying to sweep the grogginess and vivid images out of my head.

"So, these are from the late 1600s?"

11

She'd smiled as though she knew something that I didn't. But that seemed to be Flora Catlett's demeanor. She smugly tapped the small stacks of folders and envelopes that she'd placed on the wooden table in front of me. "Now, this stuff is priceless," she emphasized with a quick tap on the stack. "At least to us, so be careful. But this was that crazy period when the religion was unstable, relations with the local Indian groups, unstable, and the people were just about terrified of their own shadow. Well, I guess they would be. Mortality was through the roof," she rambled on with much animation.

I nodded, wondering distantly if this was a waste of time. I didn't really care much about who was planting what and what the climate was like three hundred years ago. "What kind of documents did you say?"

"Oh yes, maps, journals, church documents. I took the liberty of pulling out some of the juicier stuff. But you're free to look at anything in the museum." She stood up, smiling a bit smugly as though she'd benevolently given me the keys to the kingdom. And then she'd left me in that tiny office if you could call it that — one short table and two chairs at either side — slipping out and closing the heavy wooden door behind her. I pulled a small notepad out of my pocket and carefully began to examine and sort through the small pile of documents that lay before me.

Flora was right. They were old: paper parchment-like, wrinkled acutely with age; hand-drawn maps that I put aside; some wills, farms inventories, and then I stopped finding something of interest. It looked like a sheaf of papers, yellowing, some ripped slightly. But it was a list of criminal prosecutions. Thomas Fulton hanged for thievery in October of the year 1688; Rebecca Foster suspected of adultery, imprisoned. And Lucy Bonner accused of demonic influence over the children of Stephen and Christine Fulton — executed in April of the year 1689.

I glanced across the small, deathly silent room into its unadorned corner that now was not empty, was now filled with my imagination. *"What mischief can this be?"* she spoke without speaking.

I shook my head, rubbing my eyes, and she was gone. It was too quick to give her flesh in my mind yet. *"This is a strange manner of being,"* she whispered, soft small hands on my shoulders.

"I don't even know your essence yet."

"It is your choice that I appear as thus."

"What does that mean accused of demonic influence?"

Soft murmuring, *"I aided in the caring of the young ones, the children. The mother was not well."*

There was writing, affidavits further in the papers confirming what he was hearing in his mind. "Christine Fulton? But why would they think you were possessing the children?"

"It was grievous. I was innocent."

My mind traveled through possibilities weaving, "The husband?"

"He grew weary of his wife's state."

"You were lovers?" I was embellishing, of course, but it was a story, so it didn't matter.

"I had reached my 16th year, and he was a man of thirty."

Not lovers, "So, he pushed his attentions on you?"

There was silence. Then the soft floating whisper that he knew quite clearly wasn't real, just a product of his wild writer's imagination. *"Forced Peter McQuade, forced."*

"The scandal?"

"He was a magistrate in the town." His hands brushed over the old parchment confirming this. But which came first, the knowledge or her soft whisper?

"So, you were framed and innocent?"

13

"It was a diabolical calamity."

I pulled my mind away from the museum and focused on the ceiling fan above me, white ceramic with small brass accents. Well, this was good news and bad news. Finally, something had taken root and fired up my imagination. Flip side was now it was invading my dreams. It clung to me still, the rank smell of the gathering — people garbed in heavy dark clothing, the sun shining down mercilessly, and, of course, paramount was the girl — shaking from her torture in the river and then facing the tree. The short scaffold was built right up beneath where they literally dragged her, her feet painfully scraping along the splintering wood.

My stomach flipped in nausea. Lovely, for not the first time, I thought about cutting all this short, forgetting this project, and heading home to my lovely familiar city with all its people and things around me that comforted and made sense.

Impulsively, I picked up my cell phone and retrieved a number I'd only used once before.

"Hello."

"Annie." There was a hesitation. My eyes focused on a blur outside the sliding glass doors at the end of the den.

"Peter, what a nice surprise."

"What are you doing?"

It moved, and there was a blur of long black hair, long black unbound hair. She had her back to me, looking out to the river. "Right now? Actually, grading papers, and then I was going to get something to eat."

"How about we do that together?"

"Now?"

She didn't turn around, just moved away from the deck down the stairs, heading toward the river — the river that her spirit haunted. It wasn't something I could actually see. It was only in my mind, which seemed so content just to wrap around her image.

"Okay, I'll meet you at Lea's. Do you know where it is?"

I frowned. Still not a date, but what self-respecting man would set up a date at the last minute like this anyway?

"All right, I'll meet you there."

Annie Davenport

Chapter 3

She looked like a schoolteacher just now. Hair pulled back in a ponytail, glasses, a light short-sleeved sweater, and blue jeans. Or maybe she looked like a college student. I was torn between impressions. Lea's was a cozy, family-style restaurant but comfortable that I had frequented more times than I could count since I'd moved here. As it went, the food was pretty good, and the people friendly.

She took off her glasses after perusing the menu and then gave me a somewhat removed smile. "What's on your mind, Peter?"

"I'm looking to be distracted. I'm a bit on overload right now," I confessed.

Glancing around, I noticed the place was pretty empty tonight. Evidently, Tuesdays weren't their busiest time. I wondered distantly what exactly people did on Tuesdays around here. "That sounds intriguing. I'd love to hear about it," she replied, bringing my attention back to her lovely face.

I rubbed my chin. My usually well-kept beard didn't feel all that well-kept just now. "I'd rather hear about your day."

Annie Davenport eyed me curiously. "My day? Well, I taught two classes this morning, spent the afternoon at the paper trying to put it to bed, then went home to grade papers, very exciting stuff. Oh, Pam, my assistant editor, suggested I get you to write a column for the paper, nothing too demanding. Just an outsider's view of the area or really whatever you want."

"How about a historical piece?" I shouldn't be doing this. I could feel it in my bones, but something odd was driving, pushing me.

Her blue eyes focused on me strangely. "About what exactly?"

"I don't know. Maybe about how the people in this town used to hang innocent women for witchcraft."

An odd expression that I found a bit difficult to read crossed her face, then there was a perceptible sigh. "So, how did you spend your day, Peter?"

"I saw Flora Catlett."

"At the museum? I see, and now you think you know everything about everything in this town. Look, every area has unpleasant histories. I'm sure your hometown New Orleans is full of them."

"Yes," I agreed. After all, this was undeniable. "You've got that right. I don't know. Why does this feel worse, more bizarrely personal?" Why did I say this? I sounded incoherent, even to myself.

"You mean the Lucy Bonner thing," she replied slowly. I nodded, a little amazed at how quickly she pinpointed the issue. "Is that what you're writing about?"

"I'm not sure yet. How do you know about her?"

She shrugged. "I've done some digging myself. I had one of my classes writing essays about historical events, and I stumbled across her in research — not so hard to find, really. I imagine Flora gave you papers specifically about her. She's a bit obsessed as well."

I was feeling a little stunned and a bit like a chump, wondering if Flora Catlett just threw this into my lap so I'd bite. "It was quite a horrific event."

"Yes, of course, the times were, well, more brutal. But as awful as it sounded, would you believe it was the only case of its kind in this area? The only woman ever executed for witchcraft around here was Lucy Bonner."

Now this definitely hit me as a surprise. "That sounds a little implausible."

"I know, but it's a fact," she stated a tad dismissively. "Sure, there were plenty of accusations from what I understand. But they never followed through. It wasn't like up North in Salem. It was really just the one." My head was swimming, and I realized my appetite had fled as I looked down at the menu. "Are you all right, Peter?" she asked with genuine concern.

"I don't know. Something has gotten hold of me."

I could feel her hand softly touch mine, and I looked up. "You might want to think about going home, Peter. This place," she began, but then she stopped. "It's not for everyone you know."

And then I looked down at her hand, long, elegant, unmanicured, but perfectly shaped nails. "That's an ominous thing to say," I murmured, impulsively grasping her hand in mine. But then again, she had opened the door. She looked up, surprised at the contact or rather shift in intent.

"I mean, it's difficult for some people to make the jump from living in a big city to a small town. Some people just aren't meant for it."

I laced my fingers in hers, and she watched almost with a focused curiosity. "And why are you?"

"I know how to step back, be involved, but retain a distance," she admitted. And then she looked up at me with blue eyes, bright. "Most people don't notice it."

"They're happy with the veneer."

"They're comfortable with it. But you're different, Peter. I knew that from the beginning. You don't hide. You simply are."

The waitress approached the table, and Annie pulled her hand away in reflex, it seemed. The woman was gray-haired, maybe in her sixties.

Annie smiled up at her, "Hello, Helen."

She smiled back in response with welcome. "Well, Miss Annie Davenport, it's been a while since I've seen you here."

"I know. I've been so busy. This is my friend Peter McQuade."

Yeah, everyone knows everyone around here. It seemed inescapable. Maybe she was right. I just wasn't cut out for this.

"So, when all this is over, you should come to New Orleans."

We were past the main course and into two pieces of apple pie and coffee. Somewhere along the way, my appetite had resurfaced with a vengeance. "You know, I usually don't have coffee after a meal, but I like it. Is that a New Orleans thing?"

I looked up, grinning. She seemed so soft and genuinely affable, but no one could deflect something she didn't want to talk about as artfully as Annie Davenport. "Hmm, let's see. Yes, I suppose it might be a custom there, but surely not the only place, and you didn't respond to my proposition."

She glanced up from her pie with a quizzical expression on her face. "Was that a proposition?" she smiled teasingly, how she did like to hold me at arm's length but also dangle her lovely self at the end of that arm.

"Are you going to answer me?"

"Oh, about visiting New Orleans when all this is over. When what exactly is over Peter McQuade? It sounds as though you are in some sort of ordeal."

It hit me oddly, her evaluation of what I'd said. An ordeal? It was true enough. I'd written many books over the years, and each had its manner of process, its own character to speak. Some were a great pleasure, while others were time-consuming and arduous. And how would I characterize this one had yet to be seen.

"I simply meant after I was finished with my book — after I've left this place."

She nodded, "That's always on your mind, I think, leaving this place. What an unfortunate way to live, just biding your time."

"Will you come to New Orleans?" I was tired of all this dancing around. It was bothersome. I was drawn to her strongly, strange quirks, mysterious nature and all.

She paused, sipping her coffee. "Well, I don't know yet. We'll just have to see."

I sipped my amazingly weak coffee. What else was there to do? Good thing I'd had the foresight to bring some coffee and chicory from back home for the mornings. "So, this works well for you, this non-committal thing."

"I guess I'm not very interested in just being a distraction while you bide your time here."

Wow, an arrow directly through the heart. Was that what I was looking for, a distraction? In all honesty, I had no idea. I was definitely living in the moment, not projecting at all what this might look like five months down the road. But evidently, she was looking at all angles and possibilities. "Some people's lives are filled with distractions. It gives them the illusion of being full."

She laughed, "That sounds lovely, Peter."

"Doesn't it?" I was tired of waiting. Patience was definitively not my strong suit. "So, what are you doing tomorrow?"

There was a brief pause of consideration. "Hmm, working, teaching, the usual."

"And after all of that?"

She smiled a little hesitantly, "I don't know."

"Well, there's a precious little grill on the deck at my cottage. Why don't you come over for dinner, and I'll barbeque us some steaks?"

"You're persistent."

"I enjoy your company. And we can talk about this column."

"I don't know. I need to go see my aunt after work."

"Fine, after that."

She nodded, although I could feel her hesitancy, "All right."

It helped to get away from it all. But now, I had to return, return to the world of constructing what was not real. I sat in the long den of Bess Greenlief's remarkably white den, off-white short shag carpet, whitish futon-like sofa, although it did have bamboo sides, white end tables with glass tops. It was light, fresh, and had a pronounced beach-like feel. And at the far end was a sliding glass door leading out onto the patio. I sat in one of her white wicker chairs and faced the door, slowly sipping a scotch I'd poured. It was undeniable. I could fight it, but I'd found my protagonist, young Lucy Bonner. I could see her now, a bit of a wild child running through the forest, hair flowing wildly about her shoulders in a tangle. Connected to —

Then I closed my eyes.

Connected to the sounds around her, I felt; connected to the spirits in the trees, the animals. I felt a peculiar pain in my chest, like a quick stab, then it lessened.

She could feel — no, more than that, breathe the life force around her. It flowed through her at the same vibration. She stopped in the forest and turned around slowly. I could see the light overhead fading, the light from the treetops eking away into the inky blackness of night.

She turned slowly, now looking at me, peering out of my creation with eyes dark, yet blue, blue not filled with light, but with shadows. "Follow me, Peter," she whispered. And she turned and began to run, run wildly in the forest in perfect communion with everything around her.

"Lucy," I whispered. But there was nothing, no answer.

REVEREND ELSTROTT

Chapter 4

"**I** was wondering if there were any more documents I could look at."

Flora Catlett was sitting behind the large desk at the back of the Kilmarnock Historic Museum. She looked a bit surprised and a bit puzzled at my presence.

"Why Mr. McQuade, I've got to admit I am a bit surprised to see you today after the quick exit you made yesterday."

"I have to apologize for that, Flora. It was a headache that came on rather strongly."

She looked at me curiously as though she didn't quite believe me. But she did stand up from behind the desk. "Well, I could have sworn you were upset. But maybe I misread. So, exactly what are you interested in?"

I sighed, deeply feeling oddly vulnerable at my admission, "Anything, anything even remotely connected to the Lucy Bonner case."

She eyed me cryptically for a moment. "Yep, it does tend to take hold of you. Follow me," she said, abruptly heading toward the back offices with a determined step. We journeyed further down the long echoing hall that I had entered yesterday. Pausing in front of a heavy white, wooden door, she opened it with almost aggression and flicked on a light switch.

The room was bright and filled with a large cluttered light oak desk and file cabinets, as well as pictures, a vase of fading flowers, and personal touches that led me to conclude rather quickly that this was Flora's private office.

Abruptly, she yanked open a drawer and started digging in a file cabinet. It was more than clear Flora was no light touch. "I take it Lucy Bonner is the subject of your next novel."

"I'm toying with the idea," I answered as non-committal as I could manage.

She stopped digging and shot me a look that plainly stated she wasn't buying it. "Look, Mr. McQuade, if you want my help."

"Yes, yes, there is something about it, the whole thing," I admitted.

She smirked, "That kind of grabs you around the throat."

Something was off here, something unnerving about her attitude, but it was much too late to turn back. I was hooked. "Yes, something like that?"

She nodded emphatically as though it came as no surprise. "Well, you're not the first. There have been other people who have passed through here that have become obsessed with the legend."

"The legend?" I asked, a bit perplexed.

She pulled a rather sizeable padded envelope out of the file cabinet, abruptly shutting the file cabinet drawer behind her with a thrust of an elbow. "Yes, this is why I keep this in here. It used to be out with the public displays, but we got concerned that it might walk away."

"Why? What is it?"

She looked at me with a hint of a self-satisfied smirk. "It's a journal, written by the church's minister. Basically, everything you would want to know about Lucy Bonner, before and after."

I allowed myself the extra beat for her words to sink in. "What does that mean before and after?"

"Before and after she was hanged, Mr. McQuade. You see, the story didn't end on that scaffold."

I stood staring at her dumbfounded and then, without thinking, held out my hand for the envelope. She hesitated momentarily, then handed it to me softly as though it were a precious treasure. "I'm lending it to you, Peter McQuade, for you to study since you'll be writing this story. Be careful with it, and make sure to bring it back to where it belongs."

I looked down at the envelope in my hands in disbelief. "Why are you doing this?" I asked, unable to help myself.

She shook her head, looking oddly a bit dazed. "I'm not sure. I think there needs to be some peace here. Maybe your writing will help. But you better make it fiction because no one will believe it's true. That's all I can say."

I nodded, wondering if I'd just hit the jackpot or had begun the first steps of *"My Ordeal,"* as Annie Davenport had described.

From the Epistle of Reverend Arthur Elstrott
April in the year of our Lord 1689.
I have no idea whose hands this account will fall into, or where I may send it, given the weak nature of my soul. But it is my wish to relay an account of the truth and that from my efforts, one day, all our hands will be cleansed of culpability in this matter.

Again, a pain passed through my heart. I breathed deeply, my hands brushing across the smooth plastic surface covering the old parchment pages that Flora Catlett, or whoever had previous possession of the document, bound together. The antiquated pages had been slipped into lamination sleeves and put into a thin plastic binder. Something inside me was reticent, reticent to move on, although I knew in my heart this was gold that I held in my hands.

I will freely admit in this account that I received encouragement from the Magistrate to support the verdict given to the woman Lucy Bonner. I will freely admit there was some disturbance in my soul over the matter.

Once the woman was executed, the body was covered and laid out beside the churchyard late in the day. Her parents, devout members of the community, had arranged to claim the body in the early morning as they were not present at the execution.

It was a time of great disturbance. The rapid nature of the trial and the sentence and then execution, all within the span of four days, left the community in astonishment. This place, these devout people, it was not their way to move so rapidly in a matter of such consequence.

The body was laid outside the ground of the church in a wagon covered by a blanket. The sentence alone precluded her from being welcomed onto holy grounds.

But as a servant of our Lord, I must testify to the truth of things. That evening there was a storm.

I could hear it in my mind, the creaking in the tiny wooden church, the whipping of the wind outside — wildness. I tried to simply focus on the words, but they began to blur in front of me.

It was, in truth, an unquiet mind, a guilt that fueled my agitations. But I was made aware of a presence all around me, a spirit not wholly unfamiliar.

I could feel it intensely as though I was slipping into it, slipping into the skin of Reverend Elstrott. The storm was all around him, and there was guilt, such profound guilt. So, he ventured out, opened the side door to the church, and headed down the uneven wooden steps.

It felt like a rage of nature. The rain splashed wildly, and the wind blew furiously at him. No one would know.

No one would know just for the night. Already, the ground had turned into sloshing mud that his boots sunk deeply into. But he could see the wagon, not so many strides away. He pushed himself onward, in war with the elements, further out while he heard crashing around him, thunder, tree limbs. But he reached it, the wagon, and grasped its edges with his bare hands — so strange that he'd forgotten his gloves. It was as though his mind was not with him tonight. She was beneath the now-soaked blanket. So, he forced himself to reach in to grab hold of the body. But his hands pulled back in violent reflex as though he'd touched fire. But he hadn't. It wasn't fire. It was warm flesh.

I pulled back from the manuscript. Not at all sure if I had read this or if it was simply my imagination. But I scanned the document and read it over twice for confirmation.

Lucy Bonner was hung nearly eight hours before, but the flesh was still warm. I continued,

Through the unforgiving storm, I carried the body over my shoulder and brought her to lie in the church for the rest of the night. I placed the body on a small wooden table next to the side door from where I had entered. I departed then to change my water-soaked clothing in the church offices.

I paused again. It was difficult. My head throbbed from concentrating on the antiquated penmanship. I closed my eyes to clear my mind, but it was of no help. I could see it clearly, sharply, as if I were there — the old wooden church, the storm, the empty wagon outside and inside the church. I opened my eyes again because what I'd seen, I'm sure, was simply a conjuring of my imagination. I began to read.

I returned to the main hall of the church. I am apprehensive to go further. I am certain from now onward, the soundness of my mind will be in question. As a

29

testament to the truth, I will give as exact an account now as I can of these hideous events.

I returned to the hall. My sight fell on the table upon which I had placed the body of Lucy Bonner. I will admit freely my heart was filled with frightening pain and distress, and a horror stirred deep within my God-given soul.

The body, Lucy, sat upon the table. Her eyes were open wide, and her visage tainted with a reflection of wild anguish. And then her head turned, and she looked upon me. Her mouth opened, and she emitted a horrid scream.

I stopped, my heart beating wildly. That was it. That was exactly what I had seen in my mind before I read it on paper.

I put the book away. I had to. There was no choice. It was too much, too intense, disturbing all the more because of the resonance it seemed to evoke within me.

I lay down on the sofa and slept, slept hard in a fortunately dreamless sleep. I suppose it's difficult to understand why I did not read on. If this was a novel, it would have meant I had deliberately stopped right at a cliffhanger. But it wasn't, and in some very odd yet distinct way, this account was sapping something out of me. It was not only emotionally exhausting, but it was also physically draining. And yes, I can freely admit that it wasn't the first time I've experienced such a thing, but perhaps not at this magnitude. Creating stories, writing itself is a process requiring energy. There have been some projects that have felt, well, uplifting to craft, while others are a different matter. Admittedly, that was one of my ex-wife's complaints. "You spend too much time in dark places." It wasn't really so much that she was ever wrong about me, more that she couldn't live with who I was.

After the nap, I took the long drive down to the grocery to prepare for my dinner with Annie Davenport — a welcome diversion I so desperately needed.

The Dinner

Chapter 5

She looked, and the only way I could describe it was distracted. When Annie arrived on my doorstep, it was just after five. "Am I too early?" she asked, seeming more tired and pensive than I could remember ever seeing her before.

I shook my head. "No, no, come in. How about a glass of wine?"

A slow smile spread across her lovely lips. "Now that might just be perfect, Peter McQuade."

"Yes, well, every once and awhile I manage to hit the ball out of the park. I hope you like white. I know red goes with steak, but I like white."

She laughed, following me into the small galley kitchen of Bess Greenlief's cottage. "Not surprising, you don't strike me as someone who follows the rules."

I took a bottle of Pinot Grigio from the counter and began to open it. I was from a warm climate so most of my beverages needed to be cold. "Well, when you say it, it doesn't sound like a failing."

"So, I'm not the first," she murmured beside me, watching as I dug the corkscrew into the cork and proceeded to pull it out with a few twists.

"Oh no, it was one of my ex-wife's diatribes. I never tried to follow the rules."

I poured two glasses of wine and handed her one. "Considering what you do, I don't see how you could. I mean, fit into any mold." Then a bit abruptly, she headed out of the kitchen.

She was bothered by something. That much was clear, and my job was to alleviate it somehow. Or so I hoped.

Annie settled in the den in one of the white wicker chairs, thoughtfully sipping her wine. She hadn't really dressed up much for the evening, a long white button-down shirt over blue jeans and hair pulled back in a ponytail. But there was something about her, her essence, that I just found compelling and sexy. I sat across from her on the short loveseat, wondering if there was any chance I could get her to join me on it. "So, do you want to talk about it?"

Her clear blue eyes were drawn back to me from that distant place they'd been dwelling moments before. She smiled, "Not really."

"Well, that's honest. How's your aunt?"

"My aunt?" She looked at me oddly.

"I thought you were going to visit her."

The confusion cleared quickly. "Yes, I'm sorry, Peter. Maybe this isn't the best night for this. I'm feeling so out of it."

"Now you're not going to leave me to eat those two gorgeous rib-eyes I traveled so far to obtain."

"I'm afraid I won't be very entertaining."

"I don't need you to entertain me. Just be here."

She again looked at me speculatively as though maybe she didn't quite believe me. "You writers certainly have a way with the language."

"I'm sincere. And you didn't answer my question again. How's your aunt?"

Her eyes seemed to dim a bit. "She's not doing well."

A few glasses of wine over a fine meal seemed to lighten Annie's mood somewhat and mine as well. I left behind the disturbing images of Reverend Elstrott's stormy nightmarish encounter with the dead woman, at least for a little while.

"So, how's the book coming?" she asked, with a lovely smile that had drifted across her face as a more permanent fixture as the night progressed.

"You know, I forgot to get dessert."

"I couldn't eat another bite." She said, laughing from across the small dining table. "Now, whose dodging questions now?"

I stood up, holding my hand out for her. "Come on. Let's sit up front, and I'll freely answer anything you want."

She stood up, wine glass in hand, and allowed me to lead her to the loveseat, where I pretty much had wanted her to be all evening. She sat down next to me, seeming a bit more nervous, but I didn't mind. "I asked about the book," she murmured.

I sipped my wine, trying to figure out in my somewhat fuzzy brain exactly how to explain what was going on. "I guess you could say I am more in the research phase now. Haven't written much."

"Is that what you usually do?"

"Depends," taking another sip. "Do you want coffee?"

She shook her head, "No, I'm good." She smiled at me again with those gorgeous eyes, and I did something impulsive, which for me happened more often than not. I took the wine glass from her hand and put both glasses on the end table beside me. She looked at me questioningly but then seemed to understand as I bent near her and softly kissed her. Her hand came up gradually and touched me on the cheek as she pulled away. "Well, I wasn't expecting that, Peter."

I lightly touched her hair, "Too soon?" I asked.

She shook her head, seeming strangely confused. "I don't know."

I nodded, and then I put my arm around her pulling her closer, kissing her again, not worrying at all this time if it was something I should do.

I do question the wellness of my mind and my state of spiritual purity. In that instance, I reflected that I had been perhaps damned into some sort of purgatory for sins that had gone unavowed.

I walked to the wretched figure who continued to scream in abandon. Her matted wet hair draped across the pale face I once had known as Lucy Bonner. And as I came closer, I marked the bright red swollen scar across her neck created by the hangman's rope.

I compelled myself to touch her, grabbing the shoulders and shaking. "Lucy, Lucy," I implored. "How can this be?" And mercifully, it stopped screaming and looked at me with eyes of terror.

It opened its mouth, but the voice came as a horrid, rasping whisper. "Why have you done this to me?"

I pushed the manuscript away. It was too much, actually flipping my stomach with nausea. It was more than clear to me that Reverend Elstrott was demented in some way, schizophrenic, delusional. That was the only explanation. I sipped the coffee that I'd put on once Annie had left. It was after eleven. Of course, it would keep me up, and I was foolish, foolish to—

I stood up, walking across the room to the sliding glass doors, staring into the pitch-black night. There was no light anywhere to be seen, except perhaps from a sliver of a moon that might be hanging in the sky. I felt the effects of the old Reverend's epistle hanging over me like a film of sweat. I actually felt as though I needed a shower. I allowed my mind to drift backward to more pleasant but perhaps equally frustrating thoughts.

There was something mysterious and terribly exciting about Annie Davenport. Holding her in my arms, touching her, kissing her, ignited a fire in me that I don't remember having, well, in some ways, ever having before.

There was no thinking involved, just kissing her passionately, which admittedly she returned with fervor. And then I wanted more, needed more, to quell the restlessness that seemed to be eating me alive my whole life. Without a thought, I started unbuttoning her top with deliberate intent. But rather quickly, her hands caught mine. "Peter, I can't."

I kissed her again, not wanting to acknowledge what I'd heard. It was like fire, intoxicating fire that I didn't want to end, just wanted to pursue it to its natural course. "Stay with me," I murmured against her neck — soft, sweet skin I ran my mouth over.

She pulled back, stronger this time. I could feel the change in the body I was embracing, stiffening. "I can't. I'm sorry."

I still held her close, but the words had the desired effect, cold water splashing across my indulgent nature. "Okay," I whispered.

And then she did the unthinkable, pulled away completely, and stood up, walking across the room and buttoning the shirt that I had only moments ago undone. "I'm sorry," I said, knowing, of course, that wasn't true at all. I wasn't sorry in the least, and if she'd only change her mind, I'd drag her to my bed and make love to her all night.

She turned around, looking at me with all I could describe as confusion. "No, I just wasn't expecting things to go this way, not so fast."

I stood up, crossed over to her, and took her hands. I still needed some contact. There was a strange sort of electricity in her skin that I craved. I smiled, "Well, I'm a fast worker." But she didn't seem amused. She was caught in some serious place where all this meant something perhaps different to her than to me. I let go of one of her hands and softly brushed her hair — thick, wavy blond hair. "I'm sorry if I pushed things too far. I'm just beginning to get a little crazy about you."

She looked at me with an odd concern, "It might have been simpler if we'd just stayed friends, Peter."

"Is that what you want, simpler?"

Of course, she didn't answer, as was her way of not answering those things that she felt were too uncomfortable. She didn't stay much longer, not addressing what had happened and pleading an early morning. I walked her out to her car in the stillness of the night and, of course, as was my way, did push things a bit. I pulled her into my arms and then kissed her again. Softly whispering, I told her, "I'll call you tomorrow." She didn't answer, just nodded, then drove off into the blackness. That was the thing about being so deep in the country at night. Everything around you, excluding the fireflies, felt like blackness.

THE THREE

Chapter 6

There was madness in its eyes. I placed a blanket around her form to quell the trembling. "Why, why?" it rasped. "He promised me life, life always. Why has he abandoned me?"

The thing was frantic, but the very words condemned her in my mind, as did her uncanny return from death. I had been plagued with doubts at the accusations of witchcraft lodged against the girl. But here, here was the proof out of her mouth, out of her flesh. She had consorted with the devil and used that power to return from the grave. She thrashed without purpose upon the table.

With terror having taken hold of me, I stroked her hair to still her. I whispered, "Quiet child. Your parents are coming to retrieve you on this morning. You must be in stillness."

For a time, this calmed the girl. A path was forming in my mind. I acted with haste. I walked behind her, reaching into a cupboard built into the wall of the church. There my hands fell upon what I sought. Tools were kept there for varied purposes.

It was my chosen path as an elect of God's will. I would act mercifully without seeing her eyes. I took the heavy sharp instrument and moved behind Lucy Bonner. I placed my hand on her trembling back, still covered by the blanket she'd been wrapped in upon her death. "Pray, my child," I told her.

I saw her bend her head in repose. And with all my force, I plunged the large knife deep into her body. There was no sound, no scream. She slumped forward, and I pulled out the instrument, watching the body fall over onto the floor. It was far too late to save her soul, but perhaps I could protect ours from this demon.

Again, I felt sick as I closed the binder. No more tonight, no more of this. I leaned back in my chair, closing my eyes for a moment, then allowing them to flicker open as I detected a movement across the room.

"Are you afraid of me now?" a whisper, a shadow.

There was a glaze over my eyes that I did not attempt to clear.

"No."

"Are you afraid of anything?"

I considered this, pondered. "Yes," I answered.

The shadow moved, and my imagination sprang to life — same dress, same long black hair, but wet, stringy. The neck of her dress was opened enough for me to see the blazing red, welted scar around her throat and just below her waist, the spreading red stain of blood. "What are you?" I asked.

She smiled, skin so pale. *"That thing of dreams. "*

I dreamed of power, traveling, flying through substance, and then allowing it to become reality.

"Are you an angel?"

Was I? *"If I choose to be, "* I answered her in her thoughts, for she was predestined to hear me.

"Are you a demon?" she asked, but with all innocence and no judgment. The girl was not afraid of me.

"I am between," I answered. How could I explain to such a simple form how I am? The trees moved overhead, shifted as did my substance. But the mind reached up to meet mine. Not so simple a form, perhaps. *"It is dangerous for you to find me,"* I cautioned her.

And I melted back into another place.

I woke up with a throbbing headache and sat down at my laptop, beginning to write the history of Lucy Bonner. It came easily, the words like a quick-flowing river. I wrote for an hour, but when I stood up, it felt as though my limbs were trembling. It had taken something out of me. Energy again, I thought.

Almost in mindless reflex, I went to the bedroom, pulled my suitcase out of the closet, and began to pack. I had to stop. If I didn't — I hesitated, allowing common sense to filter in. I sank onto the bed next to the suitcase, trembling inside. It was no use. I couldn't stop. I was like a drug addict now, weak, with no will, nowhere to go but forward.

I closed the suitcase back up, returning it to the closet. There weren't many options left for me now. But if I wasn't leaving, and it seemed as though that had become the case, I had to get this over with. I had to understand what had happened.

It was early morning, around six. A pot of coffee and several aspirins later, I resettled into the account of Reverend Elstrott. The penmanship, which had been so controlled and legible early in this document, was deteriorating. So again, I questioned if this was simply a reflection of the madness of his mind.

We are three in this matter: one, Arthur Elstrott, Stephen Fulton, the Magistrate, and George Warren, the constable. I summoned the other two early on this morning, informing them of the night's events. At the start, both questioned the truth of my words. But now they stand convinced. The Magistrate intercepted Lucy Bonner's parents and compelled them to leave the body in our care.

It was promised to bury her on the church grounds secretly. I do not know the particulars of what was said, but Stephen Fulton persuaded the poor couple.

This night we three meet in the church. The body of Lucy Bonner has been stored in the back room, bound with rope. I have to confess that early in the morn, there was a color to the skin and a stirring of life. It is not possible, except through some wicked enchantment, that one could survive two blows of death.

I have prayed upon the matter and am convinced we do our Lord's work.

I closed my eyes, feeling a chill of dread gripping me. And I could see it manifest before me — the three men in the church conspiring, all shaken. I wanted to scream at them to stop, to recognize what they were doing, as though it were taking place now. But it wasn't. It was so long ago. I could hear the terror in their voices, skin pale and hands trembling. But the night outside was calm, not like before, no storm, just calm, stillness.

I have convinced myself that I am not damned.

The tall bearded man unwrapped a cloth on the table. It was an ax, a great ax.

She is no longer the child I have witnessed growing up in our midst.

A great heavy ax, rusted, reeking of its toil.

It only has the face of Lucy Bonner. It has become a devil.

I could see inside the locked room. The body on the floor was quiet, but the eyes, large eyes, flickered open. "Can you save me?" Thoughts were sent out, the mind wildly panicked.

And then I could feel something else, another presence, another voice. *"Sleep now, child. Sleep now."* And her eyes closed, even as the door of the storeroom was flung open.

There was no stirring of wakefulness. The only evidence of life was the warmth of its skin. They demanded I witness. We three be bound in this matter. Each one of us took a turn in the deed, swinging the ax. There was no sound, just a horrible twitching of the corpse and the blood that ran warm as though it had first been shed. We buried the remains on the church grounds, as promised, beneath a great tree. I pray for the eternal soul of Lucy Bonner and pray I truly comprehend the will of our Lord.

And then it ended—the horror of what had occurred just ended abruptly, like the end of a story. My whole body felt sweaty and exhausted as though I had just run a great distance. It simply ended. I didn't understand, and I desperately wanted to dismiss it, dismiss it all as the product of a delusional mind, as a fiction created not unlike my books filled with wayward ghosts, serial killers, vampires at times.

"But will you?" The soft voice drifted into my mind, and I saw the figure standing in the bedroom doorway. Thankfully, enough shadows were cascading across her that I couldn't see clearly yet.

"No," I whispered aloud or to myself. "Not now. I can't take this now."

"Wouldn't you want to witness?" she murmured in a delicate voice that felt like a caress.

"Not now. I have to figure this out."

There was a soft laugh telling me that, indeed this was beyond me, beyond possibility. She moved forward, not heeding my pleas.

And the pain in my heart increased. *"I didn't feel it. I slept."*

Stains of red, red gashes everywhere that looked like they'd dried long ago. But jagged ugly scars all over her skin bore through the torn and tattered dress as though she were some macabre puzzle that had been pieced together.

"Oh God," I whispered.
But still, I heard the soft laughter.

The White Marsh Church

Chapter 7

"**W**hat the hell is this?"

Flora Catlett stared at the binder that I had flung a bit too aggressively onto her desk. It was not her usual day at the museum, but I'd called this morning, finding out she'd slipped into her office. She stood up angrily. "Hey, Mister, what is wrong with you? Do you have any idea how old that document is, and you fling it across my desk like it's the morning paper?"

I was in a rage, an inexplicable rage, born from a feeling of helplessness. "That's one of the things I want to know. Why, why would you lend me something so valuable? It's a bit crazy."

She stalked over to her office door, closing it deliberately. "Do you mind? I'd rather not let everyone hear our business. So, I take it you finished it."

"What kind of sick, messed up crap is this. Chopping a young girl into pieces with an ax?"

Slowly, she sat down again behind her desk. "I thought that was what you liked to write about Mr. Horror novel — sick, messed up crap."

I was shaking inside. This was ridiculous. I knew that much. I had no idea what I wanted except just for things to stop. I sank into the small wooden chair in front of her desk, deflated by her candidness. "Why did you give this to me, really, Flora?" My voice had dropped into a heavy disgruntled whisper.

She placed her hand on top of the binder, tapping it lightly. The flash fury that my behavior had incited in her seemed to be fading. "It's hard to explain, actually, Mr. McQuade."

It was odd. Her expression looked not secretive, not that she was reluctant to tell me, but that she was somehow confused. "Have you done this before? Lent this manuscript out?"

Slowly, she shook her head, "No, not really. For about two years, I've just kept it in my file cabinet." Her voice sounded a bit distant, as though she were trying to focus on something.

"Have you looked at it?"

Her eyes grew wider. "Not for a very long time. I haven't touched it." She shook her head. "I thought about sending it to the state museum in Richmond, but I didn't." Her voice again drifted off, a strange disconnect. "And for a while, I forgot about it."

I stared at her in confusion. She wasn't making sense. In fact, she was scarcely coherent. Perhaps Reverend Elstrott wasn't the only one afflicted around here with mental instability. "So, why did you give it to me, Flora?" I felt almost as though I was coaxing a child.

She looked at me again as though trying to recall. "I'm sorry, Peter. The truth is, until you came raging into my office this morning, I had completely forgotten I'd given it to you at all."

She looked serious, completely deadly, matter of fact serious. "I don't understand."

"I'm sorry," she said, stacking some papers on her desk. "Yes, it doesn't make sense that I'd let such a valuable document leave the museum."

"Where was the church?" A completely random connection, it just popped out of my mouth.

"What?" she asked.

"The church where they buried Lucy Bonner."

She hesitated for an instant, then finally answered, "Oh well, that would probably be down Highway 54. Another church was built in the same spot around fifty years ago, but it's just a ruin now — the White Marsh Church."

Everything was a long rural drive to get to this part of coastal Virginia. My car traveled down a lonesome highway 54 that I'd located on a map since my GPS rarely seemed to work in this area. I felt driven but driven to some unknowable end. There were houses along the way, rustic type wooden frame houses, that I could easily imagine being the same a hundred years before but few and far between. Farmland, yes, but forest also encroaching, forest that oddly felt familiar.

Nearly to the end of Highway 54, she'd said, right at a junction with Sugar Hollow Trail. These names I had to remember. No one could make this stuff up. And I slowed down my old SUV that had courageously made the drive from New Orleans as I did indeed begin to approach a structure off the side of the road. As I got closer, I noted that it indeed was labeled by a wooden sign in front — White Marsh Episcopal Church.

There was a parking lot, overgrown a bit, but definitely still there, that I pulled into. Then I stopped, just turned off the car, looking in confusion at what was left of the crumbling structure.

"This cannot be."

"Has she moved?"

"No, but the flesh, it is warm."

47

The voices, the whispers, were ricocheting around in my head. All of it was leaving me in a state that was a bit incoherent. I stepped out of the car, almost at once feeling a dizziness wash over me. And oddly, at the same moment, it seemed as though a great rush of wind swept through the trees surrounding the crumbling masonry of the old church as though a storm were approaching. But my mind reminded me succinctly that the sky overhead was blue and placid.

"They did not see."

I heard it in a whisper, a whisper I could easily attribute to my imagination, and tried to desperately. It was a soft light voice. Was it behind me or in my head? But there was more. I could feel her breath, warm breath on the back of my neck. *"You showed me the way."*

I shuffled even closer to the building, my feet feeling reluctant to move forward. Where once there probably had been a wooden door was now a large jagged, gaping hole. I knew, of course, my mind knew that this was not the same church. This was not the same church where Reverend Elstrott was minister of his flock, where he'd laid down the body of Lucy Bonner. I recognized all these things, but my head pounded, and my vision blurred as I passed the threshold.

The floor beneath me felt unstable, decaying, and rocked beneath my feet, but my head, my head continued to be filled with murmurs, whispers. Was this what insanity felt like?

I could see them now, or could I imagine what had happened?

"Give me the ax quickly. Let us be done with this." Stephen Fulton nearly tore it from the hands of the Reverend and swung viciously.

"I was already gone," she whispered at the back of my neck, pushing me deeper into the church. The inside

was deteriorating as well, with great stretches of mold across the ceiling, dust, and debris, but the lines of wooden pews where the congregation had once gathered were still present.

"It is done. It is done." It was the younger man who whispered in a throaty, terrified voice.

"No, he must swing as well."

I shuffled closer to that place where they were, but now it was only a church wall, a stone church wall. But I could hear clearly, as though all of them were directly in front of me.

"Please, let us be finished," the older Reverend whimpered.

But the tall, dark-haired man forced the bloody ax into his hands. *"Forgive me,"* the old man rasped weakly and swung once.

My head swirled with sickness, and nausea flowed through me.

"I was not there anymore," she whispered in my mind. *"You had already shown me. But if they had not done this, I could not have touched them at all."*

Again, my vision swirled, and I felt distantly as though I was supposed to see something. The wall faded away, and I could see, could see the three men standing in front of the bloody remains they had further desecrated. But on the side, just on the side of them, she was standing, watching silently, just as she had been in my den, scars of violence all over her. But they were blind to it.

The old Reverend let the ax slip from his fingers to the floor. "We must bury her now on the church grounds with speed." He glanced around frantically, could feel her, I knew, because these were things I was supposed to know — could feel but not see. The girl's form moved toward them, behind them. Her hand was outstretched and reached right through the back of Fulton. He grimaced a bit as though pain had seized him. And she withdrew her hand, which seemed to hold the phantom image of a beating heart. She looked at me with curiosity. *"Do you understand? They gave me the power."*

I closed my eyes as dizziness rushed over me. When I opened them again, I was sitting in my car as though I'd never left it.

AUNT ISABELLA

Chapter 8

They sat in a sunny little nook of the long cool, white hall of the nursing home. Annie Davenport watched the elderly, bony hands of her Aunt Isabella maneuvering her knitting needles as though she were still twenty-five. Her aunt was a hair's breadth away from being legally blind, but she didn't need her sight to create with the yarn — and the long pair of silvery needles that she remembered her using when Annie was only a child and Aunt Isabella was still a woman to be reckoned with.

Although to most, it would appear the old woman's day was done, perhaps those with a trickle more of insight might perceive something different. "You know, I can still teach you, young one."

Annie laughed, "Sorry, Aunt Isabella, I've tried. I just don't seem to have the talent for knitting."

She was so frail now, slight, dressed in a day gown and long bluish robe. Her hair was thinned, silvery gray, pulled back into a bun. Her aunt didn't want it cut, although Annie had certainly offered to have it done. "You need to take up some kind of needlework then or sewing. It's important for a woman to create, to weave. It helps our souls grow."

Annie smiled, "I sew a little. I made some curtains."

Aunt Isabella rocked in her chair, still wearing the furry blue slippers Annie had bought to match her robe. "That's good. It helps equalize the mind."

Annie knew some people would think her aunt had slipped into some sort of dementia with the comments she made. But Annie had known her for a very long time, and everything she said, every little remark, was not without purpose. She waited patiently, looking out the picture window at the lovely, landscaped garden just outside. "Would you like to take a walk outdoors?" she asked gently.

Her aunt shook her head and continued to rock while her hands moved fluidly like she was playing an instrument. "Has he found you yet?" she asked, her voice distant as though to no one in particular.

Annie answered softly, expecting, well, something. "Yes."

Her aunt nodded in acknowledgment, and Annie could feel it somewhere along her skin. "Things have been stirred already, my child."

"I know," she swallowed on a painfully dry throat. She wasn't at all sure if she was ready to talk about this, but here it was upon her, ready or not.

"It is difficult to see yet, how it will go. But you must be strong."

"I know," she murmured. Then she stood up. "I'll go get you something to drink." Annie began a slow trek down the long bright hall, hearing her footfalls echo behind her. She wasn't ready, wasn't ready to confront any of this yet. But what was clear was that events weren't waiting for her.

It was mid-morning when she left the nursing home. She hadn't decided whether she would go into the paper today. There was work to be done, editing, layouts, phone calls for donations, jobs all assigned to her as it was such a small establishment. But half a dozen times, she had thought to call in and tell them she wouldn't be coming in today. But she didn't, not yet. Things were indecisive, or rather she was indecisive. So instead, she began to drive, drive toward Lancaster, drive toward some parts unknown.

Thoughts began to filter in from the past — her marriage with Richard. *"I can't even connect with you. It's like you aren't really here with me."* Was the complaint. It was easy enough to blame him for the affair, easy enough for people on the outside to have sympathy for her. Poor Ann, how undeserving she was of such treatment. In truth, there had been so much of herself that she held distant that he wouldn't have accepted. But he felt it all the same, felt the gulf between them.

She stopped the car near the side of the road. It wasn't wise. It was so deserted here, not farmland, but woods. She got out feeling the pull so strong that, almost unconsciously, she began to walk into the forest.

The trees stretched tall overhead, partially obscuring the blue sky. She heard rustling around her but continued, pushing onward, stepping across tangles of vines and roots. *"Things have been stirred already, my child."*

She began to drop her shield and let her senses expand. She could feel the movement all around her now, the shifting of energy, on her skin, in her soul. The wind swirled through the treetops, and she felt without question that it was in response to her presence.

Closing her eyes, she concentrated on the slight hum she heard around her, wrapping around her heart. There were others near. She could feel them fluctuate next to her, just a quick step across a boundary to another dimension, another level of existence. Then she opened her eyes slowly, seeing cascades of fractured energy everywhere. The sight was thick, blinding, filling her human corneas with vibrant levels of illumination that it wasn't built to absorb properly. She walked on through the rich brambles, twining foliage, all resonating with their own energy.

"Use the sight conservatively," her mother had warned. She was only sixty-five when her sight began to fail. Of course, even as clinical blindness had set in, Emilia Davenport still could see the energy through the blindness and could sense the others that walked next to them in close proximity — both spirits that had not crossed over, visitors, and those simply existing next to us in dimensions lying side by side. Her aunt's vision had only begun to fail recently. She had been brought up in the old teachings, and the bloodline of the pathfinders flowed strongly in her veins, more purely.

She wasn't sure where she was being drawn, but she continued walking, following a great shimmering path of purple through the forest. Branches were scraping her along the sides of her ankles. She hadn't dressed for a trek through the woods, just wearing khaki Capris and sandals, but it didn't matter. Something was pulling her along.

She began to hear it now, alongside the hum, water rushing along a brook of some sort. She felt it before she reached it but continued to let the sight flow through her. It burned her eyes, and the blood she felt rushing through her veins more rapidly than usual felt like a prickling acid. "Everything is accentuated. You can't stay in this mode too long, my dear," her Aunt Isabella had counseled her when she was ten. It had been the first time she'd been allowed to step into this world formally.

She stopped. She could see it clearly now, a small moving stream cutting through the heart of the forest. And just on its banks, she saw several of them at the stream's edge, white figures nearly indistinguishable in their form. But she understood this was because her human eyes could not absorb them correctly. She moved closer, then paused, waiting.

She understood quite well now how Lucy Bonner might have mistaken them for angels and how she must have felt. One moved toward her, and her eyes filled with brightness.

New Orleans

Chapter 9

I collapsed on the sofa at Bess Greenleaf's cottage, exhausted, nauseous, completely drained of energy. Forcibly, I blocked everything out of my mind, unable to fully comprehend — who was I kidding — unable to comprehend at all what was happening. I desperately tried to sleep, but it was not restful. It was a heavy sleep packed quite full of disturbing, nightmarish images.

I could see them afterward, the three men again from the church — the three men who had hacked the remains of Lucy Bonner into pieces.

First, it was Fulton, returning to his home and his wife. Just in leaving the church, there was an actual change in him physically. He'd become more gaunt, brittle. His skin actually had an unhealthy pallor. Whoever said that misdeeds didn't take their toll clearly hadn't seen this guy. And then, I could see ahead, like some sort of compressed time span. Every night afterward, she would be there, unseen, like some sort of bizarre vigil, literally reaching into his chest and pulling out pieces of his life force.

It was confusing, dizzying. I had felt such sympathy for her plight, but now she was the aggressor. Her words echoed, *"But if they had not done this, I could not have touched them at all."* Was this possible that their actions had made them vulnerable to some sort of supernatural retribution?

And then the next, the constable — it was the same, but for him, it took longer. He was not quite as easy for her to drain from, a slow drain of his energy until his body collapsed in on itself.

Then there was the last, who I felt to be the purest of the three — Reverend Elstrott. Oddly, I felt that the greatest crime was that he was weak and confused by the extraordinary circumstances. But, of course, that did not seem to protect him. I could see him clearly. Every time he preached to his congregation, he would raise his eyes, seeing her slight form walk right out of the shadows of the corner, staring at him with those eyes filled with horror. The same eyes he'd seen when she first reanimated.

Reverend Elstrott's purgatory was almost more torturous. Slowly but succinctly, it was driving the old man insane. He withered over what seemed to be several years. Every night without fail, she would visit him and not touch him — just haunt his waking and sleeping hours. Until he begged, quite out of his mind, begged her to finish it. And she did, reaching into him and pulling out what little was left.

I awoke in the den, but it wasn't a real wakefulness. It was a state of in-between. She stood there staring down at me, watching — not scarred as before, but as she was the first time I'd seen her.

"What do you want from me?" I whispered.

Her dark blue eyes widened, and she smiled. "I want to live again."

I woke up to the sound of my cell phone ringing. Again, I was in the den, but I was alone now, just me, no hellish visions.

I sat up and grabbed the phone. "Hello," I said, not even bothering to check who was calling. Anyone would do — anyone of flesh, that was.

"Peter."

I sat up, further rubbing my eyes. I couldn't believe how horrible I felt. "Annie?"

"Yes, are you all right? You sound terrible."

"I, I don't know." That's all I could say. How could I explain this without getting myself locked up?

"I'm worried about you. Do you mind if I come over?"

"I don't know. I'm not in great shape right now."

"That's all right. Maybe I can help," she said, then hung up.

I stared around the room, feeling an icy dread wrap around me. She was still near. I could feel it, somewhere very near.

Annie had called the paper to let them know she wouldn't be in today. She'd also gone into the top of her closet and unwrapped some items that she kept in tissue paper — an old book bequeathed to her by her grandmother, a black woven shawl that belonged to her mother, and a dark blue pendant whose original source was unclear. All of these she put into a tote bag she took with her.

She brushed her long blond hair and twisted it into a bun. She had donned a white dress, summery, cottony, and filmy but without jewelry. It was difficult to know what to expect.

For a moment, she stared at her reflection in the mirror she'd placed in the hallway by the front door of the small wood-frame house where she lived. There were still choices here, all sorts of choices. But then again, some she'd made long ago.

She took a deep breath, and her mind turned back to the first time she'd ever laid eyes on Peter McQuade. It was before, before he'd first come to Kilmarnock, actually several years before — around three, to be exact. She'd discovered him long before he was even aware of her existence.

It was after her divorce from Richard had just been finalized. And she was in pain — raw, unrelenting pain that seemed to chafe all around the edges of her very being. She'd been working at a paper as an editor in North Carolina. That was where she and her husband had lived until things fell apart — her envisioned life and, in some respects, herself. It was a dark, confusing time, and she'd been directionless, remembering clearly being at a complete loss of where to take her life. Her parents had settled up North in Maine, and her Great Aunt Isabella, who she'd drifted away from during her years with Richard, had lived for years in the small coastal town of Kilmarnock, Virginia. For some inexplicable reason, at that time, it was she who Annie was most drawn to in her distress.

Her aunt, who had sympathetically but rather matter-of-factly informed her that this was because it was her time now — time to start taking part in the family legacy. Slowly, she began to give her advice and directions, although they seemed opaque at the time. It was her Great Aunt Isabella who directed Annie to take a vacation, specifically to New Orleans, a city she had never set foot in; in order, she explained, to start to heal. Her instruction had been odd, but Annie was in some ways desperate and confused, perfectly willing to latch onto anything that might help.

There was, however, one specific instruction that Aunt Isabella had insisted upon fanatically. *"It's essential you wear the amulet at all times."* It was a dark blue sort of pendant that she wore with a long silver chain. She wasn't sure of exactly what the stone was, although at times it seemed to be lapis lazuli and at other times a deep sort of turquoise.

She didn't question her aunt's insistence or the instruction, which was quite unlike her, but when Annie remembered it now, she looked upon it as her time of madness. Things were done out of character. So, she docilely accepted her aunt's instruction hoping in some way that somewhere else she could find her footing in life again.

She could remember it clearly now, as though it was just happening. It was autumn, and the air was crisp, charged with an energy that made her feel awake and alive. And then she felt the pull.

It was late afternoon on her third day in the city. The previous two days she'd spent as a tourist wandering through the historic streets of the French Quarter, allowing its atmosphere to seep into her skin, her mind, stripping away the past months or, dare she say, years of stress. Her aunt had been right. There was something healing in allowing your identity just to float away and become someone or perhaps something else.

She was staying at a small quaint French Quarter hotel on Chartres Street, where she'd taken a long nap after lunch, leaving her balcony door slightly open just to let in the breeze. She awoke at about four and donned a long pastel skirt with a dark blue sweater and, of course, her aunt's pendant. She was alone, but she didn't feel that way. For a good while, she had not tried to reconnect with the training she'd received as a child and a teenager — the training that connected her with a long bloodline of special abilities, abilities to feel and link herself, for lack of a better word, to the *unseen.*

But here, this city was swimming with those familiar energies, and she allowed herself to remember — to let go of all those things she'd felt necessary to suppress in her marriage. Once she started her walk down Chartres Street, she began to relax into it, the sensations around her. She didn't allow herself to see, but it wasn't necessary. The pulls were so strong, and with a clear open mind, she followed them, followed them toward a small patio restaurant at the edge of Royal Street. She heard music, Celtic music drifting from inside. She didn't intend to go in, for it was clearly a club, but the pull was so strong, so unyielding, and she was unwilling to resist too strongly.

She crossed the patio and walked past a set of old wooden doors inside. The room was large but dim. Almost at once, her eyes felt drawn to a corner table and a man sitting there alone.

She hadn't sunk herself into the stage of sight, but it didn't matter. The energy he possessed was just bleeding out of him.

I walked along the water's edge and sat down on the steps of the short pier at the very end of Bess Greenlief's property. It was serene here. There was no touch of the stress or horror that felt as though I'd been breathing in this past week.

Again, I questioned my sanity. Perhaps, when I returned home, I should consider at the very least, a therapist. It wasn't as if it hadn't been suggested to me at times, even by my children.

"Sometimes you need someone to help you put things in perspective." That was Jessie, my pragmatic child. An anchor in some ways, but it was wrong to rely on a child for that purpose. Lily, Lily had seemed like the anchor once upon a time, but perhaps that was too much of a burden for anyone in my life.

I closed my eyes and tried to see something, anything happier, to take me away from this desolation.

She should leave. She should run, run back to North Carolina, and not look back. She began to turn, but delicate stringed music permeated the room. Her head swirled a bit in dizziness. She walked forward, not thinking, not coherently thinking at all, to a table. She would sit, sit here for just a few moments listening to the music, and then leave.

She focused forward. The singer was dressed in green, long silky green garments like the forest, and her voice felt as though it came from another place. The lovely lilting Irish tunes, melodies filled her mind, mesmerizing, making her forget, forget to think exactly what she should do.

"I was wondering," his voice was deep and familiar. She kept her eyes forward. "Wondering if I could buy you a drink."

She breathed in. And then slowly turned her eyes to him and focused, focused on seeing clearly with her human eyes, not the eyes of her bloodline.

Tall, with brown hair, a beard, and eyes— his eyes were green as well, like the singer's clothes, like the forest. And she answered without her own voice, because it felt clearly as though she were not herself. "Yes, I'd like that."

"Are you visiting?"

She nodded, sipping the mug of Irish coffee he'd seemed insistent on buying her. And it was good, warm, sweet filling in aching spots. "I've never been here before. I love the city."

He was handsome, Peter McQuade. He'd told her, and her name she'd given as Isabella Marcel, her aunt's name. Why had she lied? Good question, but because she knew this wasn't real. This wasn't real life. This was only a moment somewhere else.

In fact, it didn't feel real. Maybe it was a fantasy, maybe a dream. But how she yearned to shed Annie Davenport and be this other creature that didn't think and didn't care.

He reached across her table and put his hand over hers, and from just that contact, she knew things, so many things. The primary one was that he wanted her. Then he grasped her hand in his, and she could feel, feel forever, even though it was just a moment.

"Would you like to take a walk?" he'd asked.

She did, although she couldn't remember now what her answer exactly had been.

They'd gone up to her room. Her mind was still in confusion. This wasn't her at all, not like her at all to consider such a thing. But here she was, feeling powerless to stop anything. The first time was wild, nearly savage. It was as if they were starved for each other, seeking, seeking something beyond the physical. Then he was inside her, and something was sealed.

The rest of the night was gentler but more of the same, holding, touching, knowing each other without words. And then he'd left, promising to return. She remembered sitting there in the middle of that queen-sized bed, white sheets in disarray all around her, feeling as though she'd been through a cataclysm. Something had changed. She called her aunt on the phone, having no idea what she'd say to her, but she was in tears.

But Aunt Isabella didn't ask questions, just said quietly. "It's time for you to leave now child. Get your things and go." And she did, not looking back, not looking back, until she saw him again just over a month ago.

Annie put her bag into the car filled with the necessary items, although in many respects, she had no idea what to expect.

She felt a chill traverse her spine, a chill of recognition. She was close, and that was odd.

"She'll probably avoid you. What you are, what you represent, spells the end for her."

"But all of this seems so fantastical."

"Life in its truest sense seems fantastical. But that doesn't make it any less real."

"Your presence here will probably keep her in check unless."

"Unless," she'd pressed her aunt with concern.

"Unless she grows stronger."

It felt like a breeze passing over her bare shoulders, but she'd felt the presence. She was familiar with it, although she'd experienced it only a handful of times since she'd moved to Kilmarnock. But now, now something was different.

"It's too late," a whisper in the air over her shoulder. She braced herself. It was different. It felt somehow empowered. *"I'm closer now."* It answered, her thoughts wrapping around her like an iciness.

Steeling herself, she spoke aloud. "You need to find peace. It's time to let go."

A feeling of dread solidified in the pit of her stomach. Everything was coming together. It was as it should be, but it worried her more than she could express.

TERRORIZED TERRAIN

Chapter 10

It was ill-advised. I was certain of this. Sleeping and particularly dreaming had become a terrorized terrain, but I couldn't help it. Annie was on her way to the cottage, and the doorbell would awaken me if I could only grab a few moments just to rid myself of the unrelenting fatigue that seemed to be swallowing me.

Perhaps Lucy Bonner would relent, if only for a little while. But as it was with everything in my life lately, it was not to be.

It was the forest. More than seeing it, I could feel it all around me, a pulsating web of energy.

"Why are you here?"

I could smell the rain coming, the storm overhead, but also passing through me. Then I could sense the focal point of distraction.

The girl stood there in one spot, speaking outward as if she was aware of my presence.

"What can you be?" her voice was young but sweet.

And then I allowed my form to pass into her reality, solidifying. It was nearly painful to be here. The air was so dense and becoming solid caused pain through my frame.

"What can you be of?" she repeated, looking straight at me. This was different. I'd seen others before, but this was in between. She reached out to touch the body I'd

formed, and instead of causing pain, as I expected, I felt a surge of healing.

"You are of the angels," she pronounced.

But the surge of connection was drawing me, impossible, surprising.

I woke up with a jolt at the sound of the doorbell ringing. I heard it, but all I could do for a few moments was sit up in the chair in confusion. The dream still lingered, still wrapped around me. And to be here now instead of in it was, well, oddly disappointing.

I stood up, feeling a swell of dizziness wrap around me. Somehow, I managed to shakily get to the front door and open it. Annie stood there, waiting for me, looking quite worried.

"Are you all right?" she whispered.

I put my hand on the door frame just to steady myself. "No, actually, not really."

I sat on the couch in exhaustion, watching Annie literally pace across the den. I'd talked, talked until I felt as though I were empty of every coherent thought. And somewhere distantly, I realized that she could and perhaps should relegate me to the arena of sheer madness. It was one of my explanations as well, but I knew as soon as I saw her at my door that I needed her. I needed help. There was no handling this on my own anymore.

"When was the last time you saw her?"

Odd question, not what funny meds are you taking, or what have you been smoking. "The last time was actually in a dream just before you got here. It seems to be her favorite venue, dreams, and visions. I honestly just thought it was me at first. I do have, well, a bit of an exaggerated imagination. Helps with the writing, you know, but this—"

"This is different," she completed my thought. I felt better somehow having her here. She felt solid, as though with her very even-keeled kind of nature, she'd be able to help. Help how I couldn't begin to understand. But it was a feeling.

"How are you physically?"

"Physically?" I echoed.

She stopped and looked straight at me. "How are you feeling, Peter?"

"Oh, like hell actually, headaches all the time, exhausted, drained."

She nodded, looking at me strangely, in fact, not moving now from the center of the room, just staring almost right through me. "It's not good," she murmured.

"What? Care to elaborate?" I prodded nervously. It felt ominous, like a doctor was preparing to deliver catastrophic news to me.

She eyed me with a bit of steel in her expression, which was comforting and unnerving at the same time. "Peter, we don't have a lot of time here. So, you're just going to have to trust me." Slowly, she sat down on the small loveseat close to my chair.

I shrugged, "Okay, what exactly are we talking about here?"

She was silent for a moment as though trying to collect her words. "I'm not exactly sure where to start, so I'm going to jump in. Lucy Bonner is not a figment of your imagination. There are people here in Kilmarnock who have been aware of her presence for a very long time."

I looked at her a little blankly. She was perfectly serious. Well, at least she wasn't giving me the *you are crazy speech*. "I'm not exactly sure what we're talking about here. Are you saying she's some sort of ghost?"

"I would say that is a place to start. But what she is *is* more than a ghost, something that is trapped but has evolved on its own."

I straightened up, trying to soak this in. "More than a ghost, evolved? What exactly—"

"Peter," she interrupted, "I'm sorry. You're going to have to open your mind a bit here. I'm certain this is beyond your realm of experience, but you're going to have to accept that you are in terrible danger now."

I laughed. I couldn't help it. I tended to do that in ridiculously stressful situations. And she'd just been looking at me so direly. Now, however, at my reaction, I think she looked a little pissed off. "Terrible danger?"

"Do you want me to finish? Do you want my help?" she tacked on with a bit more emphasis.

"More than a ghost?" I repeated.

"Yes, something that refuses to move on, refuses to accept the natural course of things." She stood up and walked across the room, stopping at the sliding glass door and looking outside. "She's been this way since her death."

"Which one?" I threw in.

"Yes," she murmured. "That in itself should tell you she is no ordinary being. Her body fought its destruction, and now her soul is fighting as well, not accepting the normal course of things, rather trying to create a new one."

"And how do you know all of this?"

She turned around slowly. "We've watched her. In some ways, we've watched over her, my family — my grandmother, her grandmother, my mother, my aunt."

And then she stopped, staring at me oddly. "And you?"

"I suppose."

I shook my head. "I still don't get it. What does this have to do with me?"

"She's latched onto you and is using your creative power or, rather, your power of creation."

My head was swirling, not quite able to process any of this coherently. "I don't understand, Annie."

Her face was expressionless. "She's draining you, Peter, to become stronger. So, she can live again."

She didn't know if he believed her or not. But he was desperate. She could feel that much, desperate for anything to relieve the horror he was now living. In her experience, desperation made people more open sometimes.

She'd waited for him while he took a shower and then convinced him to pack a small suitcase and come with her. She'd told him as much as she could. It was important, though, that he understood more and that she get advice now on what to do.

Thus far, he'd acquiesced to her instructions, but he was tired and beaten down. She could feel it on her skin. He put his suitcase in the back of her jeep and climbed in the front seat next to her.

"Where did you say we were going?"

She started driving, "To see my aunt."

"I thought she was in a nursing home."

"She is," she responded. And then they drove most of the remaining way in silence.

Isabella Marcel

Chapter 11

"Aunt Isabella, I'd like you to meet Peter McQuade."

The name hit a curious chord in me. Where had I met an Isabella before? Annie's aAnt was sitting in a rocking chair in what appeared to be a private room of the Kilmarnock Convalescent and Rehabilitation Center. It was, as I would have expected, very white, very airy, and filled with well-aged seniors. Annie's Aunt didn't look toward me at all during the introduction, but then again, she'd mentioned something about the woman's failing eyesight. She simply stared forward, but her hands were moving fluidly, manipulating a pair of knitting needles and yarn in a kind of silent rhythm.

She continued to knit quietly as if undisturbed, and I noticed Annie softly closing the door behind me. "It's a pleasure to meet you, Mrs. —"

"Marcel," Annie filled in. That again struck me hard. Isabella Marcel, I remembered now. That was the name of a woman I'd met years ago in the French Quarter, a much younger woman, but to have a similar name was such a bizarre coincidence. My eyes rose to meet Annie's, but she almost immediately dropped her gaze, focusing on her aunt.

"Aunt Isabella, I've told Peter some of what is going on."

I shakily sat down on the edge of her hospital bed, wondering exactly what this old woman could possibly do to help this unreal situation. "And is Mr. McQuade accepting?" she asked softly, almost as if I weren't there.

I glanced up at Annie, who stood behind her aunt's rocking chair, hands resting on its back. She looked at me as though to encourage an answer. "Yes, I think I can accept what I've been told," I offered a bit weakly.

The old woman paused her knitting momentarily and seemed to focus on the sound of my voice. I noticed for the first time her eyes were a curious light blue color, not so unlike Annie's. "You're very weak, Mr. McQuade. Even I can see that, and I'm nearly blind. She's taken much from you already. It would behoove you to keep a very open mind."

It chaffed a little bit, Aunt Isabella's abrasive attitude, but she was right. I was the one looking for help. "Well, what I don't understand is why this Lucy Bonner is so fixed on me."

She laughed softly, not quite a cackle, not quite, and at what seemed to me to be an extremely inappropriate moment. Then she stopped, turning directly toward me now and laying those eerie light blue eyes in my direction. "I see you really don't understand Mr. McQuade. But let me be clear, through a very decisive chain of events, a very strong case could be made that you are solely responsible for this calamity we now find ourselves in."

She walked around her aunt's chair and moved to stare out the window located on the furthest wall in the small room. Her aunt was blunt, but being blunt now in such a delicate situation, Annie feared, could be remarkably disastrous. Her hand drifted down to touch the dark blue pendant that she could sense around her neck, but oddly, it wasn't there.

Of course, now she remembered, she had left it in the tote bag in the car.

She heard Peter draw a sharp breath. "What did you say?" she heard him say with an edge of incredulity in his voice.

"I said all this is your fault."

"The crazy ghost witch following me around?" he nearly rasped in disbelief.

Annie spun around. "You need to calm down," she warned him. It wasn't impossible that her aunt would refuse to help at all. She'd become more than a bit intolerant in recent years.

He looked to her, eyes blazing a bit with a measure of irritation. That was the thing about him, so often fueled by emotion. "Really?"

"Aunt Isabella, I've only told Peter part of what is going on here."

"Well, it's clear part won't do," her aunt interjected smoothly. "If Lucy Bonner were merely a crazy ghost, then things wouldn't be nearly as dire. You know you should have more compassion. This really, for the most part, isn't her fault. Many souls get lost on their journey to the next plane, become resistant, reluctant to release the flesh. These souls are the sad ones, disconnected from their spirit."

Her aunt's voice had taken on that mysterious quality that she remembered as a child when she was teaching her. It had always felt as though some greater power was working through her. Peter was still frowning, but Annie could see he was listening to her. "I thought the spirit and the soul were the same thing," he said.

"No, the soul is connected to the spirit but separate. The soul is who you are, the essence of Peter McQuade, but the spirit goes on and manifests many souls to live and evolve through. But when the soul detaches from its spirit, it is purposeless, like a lost child."

Annie could feel it, the power of his concentration now. Evidently, Aunt Isabella was reaching him on some level. "Is that what you're saying, that Lucy Bonner is a detached soul?"

"A detached soul evolving like some strange mutation into its own form."

"What do you mean evolving, evolving how exactly?"

Annie felt her stomach sink. This was the part that was essential that they'd been heading toward for years, perhaps, but now that it was here, it was like peering over a precipice. "Evolving because of an encounter she had with another being hundreds of years ago." Her aunt's voice was low and filled with conviction.

"I don't understand."

"A being from another plane of existence, Mr. McQuade, another dimension, if you will. An encounter that should not have occurred."

He was staring at her aunt as if she was speaking another language. "An encounter. What are you talking about?"

"Do I need to be more graphic, Mr. McQuade? The entity mated with her, infusing her flesh and soul with its own energy and transforming her."

"Her body? She couldn't be killed?" he stammered. His face had lost some of its color.

"Of course, not until it was utterly destroyed. But the soul, well, that is another matter. What you must realize is that our spirits reincarnate all the time on many planes of existence. You can't be so arrogant to believe the only life is on this measly planet Earth, that the only living beings are those you can perceive with your human eyes."

"Are you talking about space aliens?"

Her aunt laughed softly, and Annie could feel a pressure in her chest — a stress that she knew was not her own, belonged to him. Her aunt continued to talk, "It's so hard to release preconceptions. What a better world we would have if we only could."

"You have to try Peter," Annie began because it was essential. "My aunt knows what she is talking about."

"These other beings?" His voice sounded quaky. Of course, it was shocking, the truth, and it would be so easy for him to reject it outright.

"You've dreamed about them, about being one of them."

He stood up slowly. "How in the hell do you know that?"

"My family comes from a long bloodline of seers. The blood that runs through my veins, through Annie's, and even Lucy Bonner's, but, of course, she had no idea. She, too, was one of us. That was what made her so ripe for such a transformation."

"They thought she was a witch," he murmured.

"Yes, and I suppose all of us in those days would have been labeled as witches. But you, back then, who you were would have been considered perhaps a demon."

She saw Peter look at her aunt with disbelief and then anger in his eyes as what she'd said sunk in. "Or an angel," Annie murmured. She couldn't help it. It was what Lucy Bonner had believed.

Then almost immediately, Peter turned to her in a jolt of surprise, focusing on her with those forest green eyes that she recalled from a night so long ago. "That was what she said in the dream. I was an angel."

"Yes," her aunt muttered with a measure of irritation. "She did just before you lay with her and changed all she was."

He moved directly toward Annie, and she could feel it on her skin, the strength of his anguish. He was so close to accepting but not yet, not quite yet. "This is impossible," he spoke shakily.

Aunt Isabella laughed grimly. "Yes, impossible," and then she began to murmur beneath her breath in an ancient language that Annie had heard before, which she'd been taught as a young child, the language of the seers. Annie could hear it resonate in the room and her mind, as all seers who were on the Earth would hear. Her Aunt then turned toward him, standing up from the rocking chair for the first time and allowing the knitting needles to slip from her fingers to the floor. She straightened her bent back as much as she still could and held up a bony hand, palm facing him and throwing her voice loudly. "Clear your vision now, Peter McQuade."

Annie felt it as though something physical had impacted her and tore the breath right out of her lungs. He'd felt it too. She could see it written all over him, completely stunned, and then he turned to her. Then he stared at her — at first with confusion, then realization, then finally betrayal. "It was you. That night in the French Quarter, it was you."

THE LOST CHILD

Chapter 12

It seemed as though I was moving through a fog or perhaps a dream-like haze. What was real? My visions of the forest and Lucy Bonner or now — the jarring consequence of what this old woman had done to me, to my mind. I shook my head to simply ground myself, then stared at the beautiful, wide-eyed, now blanched face of Annie Davenport — Annie's face that I now remembered as clearly and crystallized as it had been shrouded a short time before.

"It was you," I repeated in nearly a whisper.

She couldn't have looked more impacted if I had struck her. This was the woman I'd had one night of passion with, dubiously categorized as a one-night stand. And here she was, the same woman I'd known for the past month, the same woman I had considered a friend, a confidant. "How in the hell can this be?"

"It was necessary." The old woman replied, lowering her hand and returning to her seat in the rocking chair.

"Necessary. What does that mean?"

"There's a lot going on here," Annie answered. She'd grabbed the metal bars along the edges of her aunt's hospital bed for support, looking clearly now as though she might pass out.

"Yes, well, I'm getting that. But what are you saying?"

"Your memory was clouded so that you wouldn't recognize Ann. Bonds were created, energy bonds that will help you both now and in what is to come."

I looked from one to another — Aunt Isabella's face stern but placid and Annie's guarded, eyes tearful, skin pale. "You know, I don't know much, if anything about you people, but I don't like games being played with my life."

Annie sunk onto the bed, her hands touching the sides of her bowed head. "Do you think you can handle Lucy Bonner on your own Peter McQuade?" The Aunt stated with strength and condemnation in her voice.

"What does this have to do—"

"It does. Can't you see this? All of it, all of it is connected. Exactly how do you think Lucy Bonner intends to live again, Peter McQuade? She has nobody, but she wants flesh again. She's been drawing every bit of energy she can from you to make herself stronger."

"I don't understand," I said repeating myself. It seemed to have become my mantra.

"No, you don't understand. Do you?" she rasped. Evidently, patience had run out from the old woman. "Well, let me explain it to you. She wants to live again, as you do on the earth in flesh. But has no body."

My eyes widened as a new horror crept in. "What are saying? She's looking to possess someone's body?"

The old woman glared at me with her filmy blue eyes. "Not anyone. She wants the new body her spirit has incarnated in on this earth."

I stared at her blankly for a moment. Then my eyes turned to Annie. She wasn't looking at me. She was just looking down, then slowly her bright blue eyes rose to meet mine, and I knew, I knew exactly who Aunt Isabella was talking about.

"Why can't I reach her?"

"It's complicated."

"If anyone could help her, I should be able to."

"The girl she used to be when her spirit knew her is gone. What's left is an echo of what she was. She is the lost child, the one who only knows want, gropes aimlessly for satisfaction."

"That can't be all that's left."

It was too much. Annie's head was pounding as though it were ready to explode. They were staring at her, her aunt with the blankness of her failing eyesight, and Peter, Peter in total disbelief. She stood up from the bed and felt a sweep of dizziness pass over her. Just as she began to fall, Peter caught her in his arms, scooping her up effortlessly and laying her on the bed.

But still, the blackness came over her vision, and she sunk deeply into somewhere else.

She found herself back, back in the forest near the creek. The creek and beside it, they stood, three of them.

They hadn't spoken but placed something in her mind that she couldn't remember now — something bright, burning, light that encompassed everything. Her head swam again, and she opened her eyes. Peter was standing over her. "Are you all right?"

"You need to take her home. It's been too much," her aunt's voice from across the room.

She thought to speak but couldn't, too much dizziness.

"I don't understand why—"

"Yes, I know," her aunt's voice. "Only considering how this impacts you, but the truth is she's been carrying your burden much longer than the few moments you've had to acknowledge the weight of it."

"Now look—"

"Can you take me home, Peter?" she managed that. It would do no good if he became antagonistic with her aunt. They needed her now. She shakily sat up on the bed and felt his hands on her back, warmth, energy seeping into her. "Are you sure you're all right?"

She nodded, lying. She wasn't all right, but she had to keep going. He helped her to her feet, and she allowed herself to feel his strength. He had no idea who he was or what his life could be. She reached over, picking up her purse from the bed. "Aunt Isabella, I'll call you later."

"Yes, child, and Mr. McQuade, consider carefully what you have learned here and what you do next. So many lives depend on it."

CLOSER

Chapter 13

Flora Catlett liked working in the museum after it closed at 4:00 PM. She would often stay just maybe an hour, maybe two past when everyone else had vacated to catch up on her work; or to keep working on the history of the area she intended to publish with the museum's funds. It was one of the perks of being the curator, archivist, or whatever other title she dreamed up.

Of course, her history wouldn't be dry, not at all. She had enough documents here to enliven the hard facts with personal intrigue, particularly in the early days, even before there was an official Virginia.

She sighed deeply, sipping a diet coke she'd gotten from the machine about half an hour before. Her head hurt. It had been a phantom pain plaguing her on and off all day, but now, now it had intensified.

She leaned back in her leather chair, piddling with her computer on Facebook rather than writing as had been her plan. All she needed was time for the aspirin to kick in.

Vaguely, she heard the door to her office open and close softly behind her back. Someone must have returned because she was more than certain every soul had left. She didn't turn around because she was a confident woman. She ruled the roost around here, showed it at all times, in all demeanors, and all action or lack thereof.

"Forget something?" she asked, randomly shuffling through some papers that had no impact on anything at all, but there was no answer behind her, and it did irritate her.

She thought perhaps it was Colleen, the assistant curator, or Edward, the handyman, that they'd hired to work on the new wing. She called it a wing, but it was just a long room, once a storage room they were remodeling for exhibits. But Flora liked to say it was their new wing. It sounded like they were more relevant than most thought they were.

She waited a tad impatiently, but still no answer. So, she spun around in her chair, expecting, well, expecting someone familiar.

The girl just stood motionless in front of the closed doorway, long black hair draped across half of her face. Flora felt a disconcerting tugging around her heart area and an accompanying sharp pain in her head. There was a smell that had filtered into the room, a moldy smell like something that had come out of a moist place and rotted a bit.

She cleared her throat, noting the strange, deteriorated costume that the girl wore — old vintage clothes, dark, a bit shapeless.

"Can I help you with something dear?"

The eyes darted about a bit, looking everywhere it seemed, but finally resting on her, disturbing light-colored eyes, pale blue. Then unnervingly, there was a very slow grin that stretched across the pale bony face.

"You know, the museum is closed." She said, meaning to tack on the word dear, but she didn't. She just couldn't get it out of her mouth.

A thin hand raised and slowly pulled the lank hair away from the face. It felt like a frozen moment for Flora, unbelievably horrible. There were scars everywhere. Zig-zagged, puffy red mounds of flesh that had grown back over wounds, seemingly trying to repair it. Flora felt the tightness in her chest escalate immeasurably. There was the scar, too, around her neck where, and then she knew it, where the hangman's noose had squeezed the life out of her the first time.

Flora started to cry silently with fear. She understood now. She'd read the account in vivid detail, Reverend Elstrott's account of how they chopped Lucy Bonner into pieces. And there were the scars, like an ill-fitting puzzle coming back together. "You can't be here," she heard herself say in a quaking voice.

The mouth opened to speak, but it was hoarse. Oh God, she knew hoarse from the hanging. "I am," it said.

She stood up slowly from behind her desk, praying, scrambling her mind for some way to escape. "I know you, Lucy Bonner. You can't harm me."

There was a shuffle across the floor as a torn, muddied skirt dragged towards her.

"You can't hurt me," Flora Catlett repeated. And maybe just once more before Lucy Bonner reached her hand into Flora's chest.

On the ride back home, Annie felt as though she traveled in and out of consciousness. As she closed her eyes repeatedly, having given Peter directions to her house, she knew she passed in and out of vision. Her eyes closed, and she was in the forest, running through the forest on a warm day — sky overhead blue, pale blue, the color of heaven. Then she stopped, hearing, *"I can see you. There is no hiding."*

Her eyes flickered open, and her head raged. "Something's happening," she said.

Beside her, Peter grabbed her hand. "Do I need to get you to a doctor?"

She shook her head and closed her eyes again, sinking deeper. She felt free, light as though every other part of her existence pressed unnaturally upon her. But not here. Here she was as she was meant to be.

"How is this?" he asked.

She didn't see him as a man but rather felt it. *"I have no answer. Have you come from heaven?"* She'd had the existence of divine angels drummed mercilessly into her head since she was so young. So, this must be one, but only the truly deserving was allowed to see such a creature. And she was a sinner. This she was told on a daily basis.

Then he'd reached out to touch her arm, and she felt the energy pass into her skin, her soul. *"Take me with you, please."* she'd asked.

Then the light and the touch wrapped around her.

Annie opened her eyes again. The car stopped. She felt sick, weak, nauseous. "Something's wrong. She's closer now."

"What does that mean?" he asked, holding her hand.

Her eyes widened. "She's trying to pull me closer."

Annie's House

Chapter 14

Annie Davenport's little wooden frame house was filled with light. The moment we crossed the threshold, I was overcome by a feeling of warmth and peace that, unfortunately, didn't last. She immediately disappeared into the bedroom, pleading exhaustion. I was left alone, struck with the realization that my life now rivaled one of my most intricate horror novels and, in most ways, surpassed it. Let's face it. I wasn't that good of a writer.

Annie had asked that I give her half an hour to rest, so I sunk despondently into a light green overstuffed chair. Yes, I wanted to sleep as well. I was painfully drained of all emotion, all energy, and all reason. But at this point, I couldn't handle another encounter with Lucy Bonner, not that she was in any way relegated to my dreams.

So instead, I held off sleep, allowing myself to soak up what was around me. There were paintings on the walls — lovely lush landscapes and old ornate reproductions that looked a tad Victorian. There were shelves with crystals and other highly polished, semi-precious stones and crocheted afghans flung over comfortable chairs.

It struck me in absorbing her décor how very little I really knew of Annie Davenport.

She came from a long line of witches, for lack of a better word, although Aunt Isabella had termed them "seers." I stood and walked over to a long window in her den lined with soft beige sheers. Outside, I could see a small garden on the side of the house, roses all of different shades. She was sensitive and romantic, I felt this, but it was all hidden, hidden behind a wall of defensiveness. Then I allowed my mind to roll back to that night so long ago.

It had been oddly blurred in my mind for so long, and I'd attributed it to heavy drinking, but the textures and the sensations had remained. Just details had been obscured.

I clearly remembered the feeling of being near her. It was as if I was inexplicably drawn, magnetized, to be as close to her as possible. And she'd seemed delicate to me, emotionally, I thought, but also open, accessible in a way, as though she'd felt the same need, the draw.

There hadn't been much time at all for amenities. We'd allowed ourselves to be caught up completely in the physical, in the necessity. Oddly, her face had been blocked from me for so long, but I remembered other things — the feel of her skin, soft like silk, intoxicating.

I'd held her impossibly close and made love to her pretty much through the night. It had been just one night. That I remembered clearly. It was rapturous, as though being with this woman blotted out everything that had come before and oddly began to heal me.

Then I'd left, left early in the morning, having made arrangements to see her again that afternoon. That morning she'd been different somehow, not as open, more guarded. I suppose I should have expected something was off, but again, we'd spent the night in the most intimate way. Then to my shock, as I really didn't see it coming at all, when I returned later in the day, she was gone. She had checked out of the hotel without a word, not a trace.

I glanced toward the hallway that Annie had disappeared into, and now that woman was sleeping in this house, this woman I'd known for nearly a month without a clue. Yes, this whole incredible, bizarre business certainly made me feel exactly that way, clueless.

I felt a weakness pass through my chest. Whatever I accepted or didn't accept, I felt weak, as though clearly something was sapping the strength out of me.

Annie bent over the sink in her bathroom and splashed cold water on her face. She needed to drench herself in cold water, if only to penetrate the numbness that seemed to be wrapping around her. It was important she think now, not be sluggish, not be complacent. Now was the time to act.

She laid down on her bed, feeling grogginess stretching completely over her. Dimly, she was aware of Peter in the next room. They hadn't spoken about the revelations that had occurred when they were with Aunt Isabella. She had no idea how he felt about any of it. There was so much, so much to take in.

"Why can't I remember her if she is part of me?"

"Not everyone remembers past lives, and her soul is no longer connected to the spirit."

"But I should be able to reach her."

She couldn't help it. The sleepiness overcame her, and she began to dream, dream of another's thoughts.

Dimly, she remembered, remembered the forest and small snippets of other things. She recalled the flesh, the touch of her mother's hand through her hair, laughter with her friends, and then the nightmare that came in broken, jagged flashes of horror, extreme terror, and then change.

The voices would speak to her, calling from a distance. Sometimes it was her mother's voice, begging her to remember to let them help, but then they were drowned out by the roar — the roar of need.

It was easier, easier to pull what she needed now. It made her feel stronger. And he was here. She could feel him near. She recognized him as the one who had touched her so long ago in that other life. He was near, and she pulled from him, pulled light out of him, but his supply seemed endless. Not the others. The woman had fallen apart so quickly, but she could smell others, the others who were stronger and purer.

Annie's eyes snapped open. Her heart was racing. She sat up, rushing into the front den, where she found Peter sleeping in a chair.

"Peter," she had to control herself not to scream.

He opened his eyes in disorientation as though he'd been roused from a heavy sleep. "What is it? What's happened?"

"She's hunting."

Annie seemed in an absolute panic. And even I knew from my experience that this was the time when you make mistakes. A quick shower and a cup of tea later, she seemed to have regained a measure of calm. At least, she appeared that way as I sat across from her at the small dinette near the kitchen.

"Now, you're sure you're picking up on her thoughts."

She nodded, "It feels that way. I'm getting flashes of images and sort of disconnected ramblings. There does seem to be a mental impairment going on. Reasoning is completely fractured. But that's not unusual with ghosts, souls trapped between. They can't see or think clearly."

I didn't like the shakiness I heard in her voice nor the paleness of her face. I reached across the distance, patting her hand as if to reassure her. She looked up at me, those flawless blue eyes. "I'm scared, Peter. I knew in some way things would have to be resolved, but this, this scares me."

"You need to keep your focus, Annie. Why do you think you are tapping in this way?"

She shook her head. "There is a connection between us because of the spirit, but it's been severed for so long. Now, I don't know. She's getting stronger and moving toward me, first my thoughts, then," she laughed unexpectedly, almost in a bizarre franticness. "Then the rest of me, I suppose." She sipped her tea silently, and a feeling of dread passed over me. Was this really in some way my fault, as Aunt Isabella had intimated? Was all this, for lack of a better description, my karmic burden to bear?

"I'm sorry," I murmured, feeling like total hell and over my head.

She looked up, a bit confused. "What do you mean?"

I shrugged. "Your aunt said it. I'm to blame for this colossal catastrophe. I meddled with the young Puritan girl, and now look where we are."

She looked at me blankly and then began to smile a bit. "It's not really that cut and dried, Peter. We've all had past lives where we've taken actions that we find inconceivable now. You shouldn't judge it. It is a process of the spirit learning, and karmic obligations aren't a punishment but rather a tool."

"Of learning?"

"Yes, who's to say in that past life that the involvement with Lucy Bonner wasn't supposed to happen, to bring us all together now for some unknown purpose? Life isn't about judgment of good or bad. It's about learning, about evolving."

Her words were calming, and her voice — soothing, the effect that she always seemed to have on me. "You really believe that?"

"I try to," she answered softly.

I nodded. I had to hold it together, be strong for her. After all, I wasn't the one confronting possession by some crazed ghost. No, I was just the one helplessly watching while everything was spinning well out of my control.

Again, I worked to steady myself, to be of some use. "So, where do we go from here?"

Her eyes became distant, and a fear passed through her that, somehow, I could keenly sense. "I'm not sure."

"Well, then, may I make a suggestion?"

"Of course."

"If you're privy to Lucy Bonner's thoughts, incoherent as they may be, let's use that to find out where she's headed next."

She stared at me with a measure of trepidation and nodded in agreement. "Yes, that's worth a try."

THE FOREST

Chapter 15

They sat down on the broad red and black Aztec pattern rug that lay across the wooden floor of Annie's den. Peter sat cross-legged across from her, wearing a curious expression that made her want to laugh. At times, it hit her how completely overwhelming this must seem to him. Annie couldn't imagine being in his position, having all this mystical stuff suddenly thrust upon him. For her, it was natural. She grew up with it as integral a part of her life as going to the movies or shopping at the mall had been for other teenage girls. Peter, on the other hand, had received a crash course and in many ways appeared to be taking it in his stride. Perhaps, that led credence to the theory of who he was or who he used to be.

"Now, we need to hold hands." She stretched hers out and felt him grasp them in his own. Almost at once, there was this warm strong energy, like an electrical current passing between them. It was impossible to deny the draw, the attraction that she felt for him. It was something she'd deliberately buried once he'd arrived in Kilmarnock. Her aunt had predicted his arrival, and she had doubted. She had doubted until he was here, living here.

"How can this be?" she'd asked.

"The spirit knows what it needs and will follow its path to the detriment of possibly any other consideration."

"What now?" he asked.

"You should close your eyes and clear your mind, Peter."

He smiled at her, doing as she asked. And she closed hers, allowing herself to sink into that quiet, serene place.

Isabella rocked calmly in her chair. Silence had fallen upon her wing at the nursing home as it often did. They'd asked her when she moved in what she preferred — more occupied or more secluded. She had opted for seclusion, for it wasn't as if she was really alone at all. She was so close to the transition that many visited her often, friends from the past, her parents, and her spirit guides—and these last few days had been busier than most. There was always someone with her, whispering, helping her understand all and, most importantly, what must be done.

She felt grateful for the life she'd lived and yet had no qualms in the least of the thought of relinquishing it. The future and the next world loomed so close, like a brand new adventure tantalizing her. All that was left now here was to set things in motion.

She rocked silently, facing the window, her knitting on the small end table next to her chair. She felt comfort in those who were near but not too near. They would step back now and allow her to finish things.

The door behind her creaked slightly as it opened. Isabella wondered why the girl felt the necessity of using a physical door. Then again, that was her goal now, reconnecting with the physical world. Poor child, she thought. It was a shame she couldn't appreciate the glory of finally letting go of the flesh and all the burdens that came with it.

Isabella didn't turn. She simply waited calmly in her chair until the girl made her way around to her. She sighed deeply. It was so very sad the way she clung to her mangled form, but it was a choice, after all.

She looked at her with wide, malevolent blue eyes. And she thought of how easily fear transformed into aggression once given a bit of power. But Isabella looked upon her with peace in her heart. There was nothing to fear here. What she could take, Isabella would freely give, freely give with all it had to offer.

The girl moved closer and reached toward her heart. But Isabella didn't feel anything. She was already moving toward the next doorway.

We were in the forest again, Annie and I, together this time. I'm not exactly sure how it happened. In some ways, it felt like slipping into a light sleep. Not exactly, though. There was more control, although vision had definitely changed.

Beside me, Annie looked different, dressed in a long emerald-colored dress with a bright blue pendant that seemed to nearly glow, which hung around her neck.

"What should we do?" I asked. It didn't exactly feel like words, another kind of communication.

She looked at me, smiling as though to comfort me, then began to walk forward as I followed. There was light from somewhere illuminating the forest, but overhead, I could see the stars as though it were night. The path seemed easy as I followed her, almost as if the branches and trees around somehow had made way for our presence.

It was undeniable. There was peace here. The peace was so strong it almost made me reluctant to return to my life. For honestly, what was back there for me? Obstacles, mistakes, broken dreams — the pain of a world that had become quite difficult to live in.

I continued to follow her and heard the sound of rushing water. It was a creek that I had seen in my mind before we arrived. They were waiting for us there, near the edge of the flowing water. Strange, almost a magical place, as I could now remember where both worlds mesh — where one can cross from one to another.

Annie stopped some yards away from them, but I moved forward. There were three of them, beings of light, as they'd called us, and someone else as well.

Annie moved to stand beside me and before the tall woman with long dark hair. "Aunt Isabella," she spoke.

I looked more closely. I hadn't recognized her. It must be as she was when she was young, thirty or so. She smiled warmly, blue eyes alive and electric.

"Yes, child, we are all here to help you. It now falls to you two to set things right."

Annie looked at her oddly, but her aunt's smile seemed to easily melt away her concern. "The soul of the lost one must move on. You must see that she does before more innocent lives are impacted."

I looked at the others, so familiar and comfortable that a part of me simply wanted to cross over and join them.

Their thoughts came strong. *"Take our strength,"* and I felt a massive impact to my chest as I fell backward on Annie's carpet.

Annie felt her aunt speaking to her mind, soothing, encouraging. "It's your turn now, Ann. Take my strength, my guidance, child."

She saw her smile, felt her spirit near her, and then she fell back into their world. Peter had let go of her hands, and vaguely she could feel him lying on the carpet beside her. Slowly, she opened her eyes, allowing those feelings of well-being from the forest to stay wrapped around her as long as possible. Perhaps, they were strong enough to deal with this, perhaps — and then she stopped, and the strong light from the room came filtering into her vision.

"It's your turn now," her aunt had said.

Peter was sitting up, rubbing his eyes. "I feel like I've been hit," he muttered. She turned to him, but she couldn't shake this feeling of dread that was growing in the pit of her stomach. He focused on her, touching her shoulder. "What is it?" he asked.

She shook her head and sprung up from the floor, nearly running to the bedroom, where she grabbed her cell phone. Tears had already begun to come, running down her face. She quickly dialed the nursing home, waiting for an answer.

"Kilmarnock—"

"Hello, this is the niece of Isabella Marcel. I was wondering if someone could please check on my aunt."

There was a silence at the other end, and then, "I'm sorry. We were getting ready to call you Miss Davenport. A nurse found your aunt a few minutes ago. I'm sorry. She's passed away."

She couldn't speak. It was too much. She let the phone drop on the bed as her body was wracked with sobs. She felt so alone, and then she felt Peter's arms go around her, pulling her against him. "She's gone," she managed to get out brokenly.

"I know," he whispered against her hair."

"Oh God, what are we going to do now?" She just continued to cry as a storm of fear and sadness seemed determined to take her over.

THE CENTER OF THE STORM

Chapter 16

I'd known it as well, I suppose. The moment I saw Annie's Aunt Isabella in the vision so transformed, an awareness had begun. Then once Annie confirmed it through the nursing home, it became clear. Her aunt had crossed over, but what plagued me that I didn't voice was a suspicion that there was more here.

I held her tightly in my arms as she simply seemed to fall apart. I knew it was a terrible blow, her aunt dying so suddenly, but what I felt more distinctly was that she had just given way under the weight of everything. After all, how much was one human being expected to handle before they crumbled?

I held her close and felt anguish exude from her shivering body — shivering with emotion, with crying, so much pain that I could hardly bear to feel.

So, I did what was instinctive. What I felt on some strange level would help. I grasped her chin in my hand, tilted it up, and kissed her. She seemed startled at first, pulling back a bit. Then I kissed her again, feeling that powerful connection we'd ignited in New Orleans beginning to surface again.

"Peter," she spoke brokenly.

"We need each other," I whispered, kissing her and feeling her meeting my intensity with surprising force.

Sometimes it's important in the middle of a storm to simply let the world melt away, and we had. We'd held each other so closely and made love in Annie Davenport's bed, pretending for a moment that we were simply two people lost in each other.

She'd gotten up smiling, looking oddly stronger. "I'll put on some coffee," she said as she disappeared into the front room, dressed in a short silky robe she'd pulled from the closet.

It felt right, right, and I felt peaceful as my mind began to wander in impossible directions. I contemplated just leaving with Annie now — going home and leaving this bizarre situation behind us.

I breathed deeply in momentary contentment. Then I noticed the shift in shadows in the corner of a room near an antique-looking rocking chair with a red afghan draped over it. They began to move, but maybe it was just the light. But then the chair, the chair began to rock definitively, and my breath caught in my throat.

There was the sound of breath, of a deep breath, and then the shadows mutated from behind the chair. She was different this time, more like the first time I'd seen her, long black hair glistening, her dress clean and well-fitted, her face delicate, pale, but lovely. "This is the way you prefer me, Peter," she spoke in a light musical sort of voice.

I shifted to leave but recognized I was naked beneath the sheets. "Lucy," I began. "It's important that you move on."

She smiled a bit and moved closer. "If I unclothe for you now, Peter, will you lie with me as well?" she asked.

My breath caught in my throat. Not exactly the question I was expecting. "Lucy, your parents are waiting for you in the next world."

She came closer, making me feel weaker as she approached. "I have become stronger, Peter. That is well if you enjoy her body. It will belong to me soon."

I felt a stab in my chest and opened my eyes. I didn't remember sleeping, not at all. In the next moment, Annie stood in the doorway, a look of deep concern marring her face. "I just got off the phone with the paper," she said. "Flora Catlett's had a stroke. They don't know if she's going to make it."

I got dressed, trying not to think, not to think about the possibility that loomed before me as large as a red flag waving not so delicately in the wind. Yes, I had to get back to writing, that venue where I was comfortable, where the monsters were of my creation and manageable, or so I believed. When I walked into the den, Annie, also fully dressed now, was on her cell phone, pacing back and forth across the floor. She glanced up at me once, eyes wide and concerned, and then returned to her conversation — wonderful, more bad news. It seemed to be in ample supply.

The smell of coffee led me in the direction of her rather spacious kitchen — a room I had yet to visit. It was as the other rooms had been, decorated creatively with ornaments, one of those crazy cat clocks whose eyes move as its tail swings, bright polished pots hung on the walls — a very inviting place to be. Annie had created a lovely cocoon of a home, and it made me wonder if she'd ever want to leave it. As I poured my coffee into a lovely teal-colored mug that I snatched off the rack standing on the counter, I realized that, for the first time, that was exactly what I wanted. If we survived what was to come, unfortunately, that felt like quite the "if" right now, I wanted her with me in New Orleans. We could eat beignets, listen to jazz music, and stroll through the French

Quarter at odd hours when it was devoid of crowds. And live, just live.

Then she walked into the kitchen with a grim expression, and my fantasies fled under the pressure. "Do you have sugar?" I asked before I asked anything else. I had a feeling I needed that belt of caffeine to handle whatever was coming.

She pointed to a lovely rose-colored ceramic bowl that had escaped my notice. I'd already found a spoon and began to doctor my coffee. "I just got off the phone with the nursing home."

I nodded, stirring my coffee and oddly knowing what was coming. "They're suspecting a stroke with my aunt."

"Like Flora Catlett," I murmured. And then I remembered what Lucy had told me not so long ago: *"I've become stronger now."*

I sipped the coffee. Bless Annie. She'd made it strong. I leaned back against the counter, trying to figure out exactly how to tell Annie what I suspected. But as it went, I didn't have to. "You think it was Lucy, that she had something to do with this."

"I had a dream about her after you left the bedroom."

"What happened?" she asked a little shakily.

Another sip, "Well, it was still in the bedroom. I didn't actually realize I was dreaming. She said she was getting stronger. She said—" Then I stopped.

She looked at me oddly. I'd swear an eyebrow rose like Mr. Spock from those old Star Trek episodes. "She said?" she repeated flatly.

"Essentially, I think she was coming on to me and said if I liked your body, that was good because it would be hers soon."

There was a pause for a moment with no reaction, then simply, "Lovely," she murmured. "If I weren't so frightened, I'd be really pissed off."

I put down the coffee and took her into my arms. "We've got to stay strong here, Annie. Your aunt —"

She pulled away, "How could she cause them to have strokes?"

"I think it might be energy. She's found a way to pull massive amounts of energy from them, and it's too much."

She nodded, "But what do we do?"

Again, I pulled her into an embrace, having no idea what to say.

Surrender

Chapter 17

She watched. She was near them, but they couldn't see her. It took a great deal out of her to have them see her. Lately, it was much easier. She'd been alone for so long. At times, it felt only like a moment. She would sleep, dream of another place filled with light, and those she remembered who loved her. Then it would be gone, and she'd be cold again. So, she watched them and wanted. It was a terrible thing to just want, like something digging at your insides.

The whisper again, *"Lucy."* It was probably her again — the one with the blue eyes. *"Lucy,"* the old woman said. She'd thought she was gone, but she kept turning up beside her.

"Why are you here?"

"To help you."

"You can't."

"What do you want?"

She looked around at them again. She could see them through the haziness. What did she want? She just wanted. She was want. That eternal need that stabs. "I want to be there."

"Then be there." The voice whispered.

It was getting late. It had been an incredibly long, nightmarish day. Peter had suggested they shelve everything and start fresh in the morning. In the morning, she would have to make arrangements for her aunt. Her body had been taken to a funeral home in town. They'd asked her if she wanted to see the body, but she remembered what her aunt had told her. *"The body is only a vessel, a skin for the spirit. Once the soul and spirit have departed, there is nothing left."* So, she'd declined. Tomorrow she would say goodbye. Peter had gone out to get something for dinner. He'd been reticent to leave her alone, but she told him to. In fact, she'd insisted. She needed time.

Annie stared at her reflection in the mirror — eyes red, face pale, but expression determined. So, she waited.

There was a rocking chair in the corner of her bedroom where she sat down. It reminded her of her aunt. *"It's your turn now Ann,"* she'd told her. And it had come to her slowly, exactly what that meant. She tried to clear her mind. She had to be strong, had to focus.

"A lost child," her aunt's description had drifted across her mind as the figure of Lucy Bonner moved out of the shadows. She'd never actually seen her before, just glimpses in dreams. But here she was, in some ways, looking quite vulnerable to her — so young, not bearing the scars Peter had described.

"You have to stop now," Annie directed toward her mind or rather the fractured impression she could feel of her mind. It was chaotic, definitely resembling some sort of insanity.

"No, I do not." It spoke. No, she spoke. She must let her know she was acknowledged. Whatever she'd become, she was acknowledged.

"You must stop hurting people."

She looked like a child, a frightened young girl to her. She should hate her. She should be afraid, but all there was now was pity.

"I hurt," she said in a raspy whisper.

"It's all right. Don't be afraid." Her aunt spoke to her. She was so close to her in her mind now.

"I don't want you to hurt," Annie said. Then slowly but deliberately, she held out her arms to the girl. And the girl moved closer to her, closer, and she deliberately did not bar her way.

It was nearly seven. It would be getting dark soon, and I was feeling unbearably anxious. Annie had nearly insisted that I leave the house. It caught me completely off guard. It was confusing and strangely disorienting. A part of me wanted to stay at her side, protecting her every moment, but something else was pushing me strongly to acquiesce to her wishes. I suppose I could understand. A lot had happened, her aunt, Flora, all the revelations about Lucy. And truth be told, she seemed calmer and more determined, assuring me as I left that everything would be fine.

But now that I was out here, a slow panic was growing in me. It was ridiculous leaving her home alone, reckless on my part. I gunned my car's engine, trying to return as quickly as I could to her house. Annie's car was still at the nursing home. We'd decided to wait and pick it up tomorrow. After all, there was paperwork and —

I pulled up into the driveway of her house and turned off the car. Beside me was a bag of sandwiches that I'd picked up from a local restaurant. It was the oddest feeling now, just me sitting in the driveway, caught in some sort of paralysis. My heart sank, and my hands trembled on the wheel of the car. I didn't profess to be a psychic, but I knew in my gut that something was terribly wrong. Something oppressive was coming from that house now.

"Oh God," I muttered to myself. I was such an idiot. How could I have done this? I should have never left. Why did I—

"Stop," the voice whispered in my mind. I recognized it at once, the inflection. *"She must learn Peter McQuade. And it's your job to teach her now. Don't fail."*

I grimaced. It was Aunt Isabella from the great beyond, still giving me a hard time.

Journey into Darkness

Chapter 18

Annie had given me her keys, so I let myself in, not knowing at all what I would find. I had to wing it, fly by the seat of my pants — something I actually wasn't unaccustomed to. I didn't think too much, didn't think at all, didn't plan, just walked into the den and dropped the bag of food on the dinette table.

She was standing at the far end of the room, her back to me, staring out a window. She turned around slowly, and I realized that she was in that white dress she'd been wearing earlier. But I clearly remembered that she'd changed. And she now wore that strange blue pendant on a chain, the one I remember from New Orleans. She looked at me with no expression but with Annie's beautiful face and Annie's warm blue eyes that weren't warm but distant now.

I walked a few steps closer, feeling all over my skin what had happened. I wondered if my heart had stopped. It certainly felt as though it had. "Are you going to try to pretend?" I asked calmly, amazing myself. Of course, I couldn't summon any emotion. The ground had dropped out beneath my feet, and my world had turned into inescapable madness in a fraction of a second.

She tilted her head to the side ever so slightly, perhaps in puzzlement or maybe amusement. But I didn't know because I didn't know her. I knew how to read Annie instinctually, but what was blatantly clear was that this wasn't Annie. "Is that what I should do?" she asked in a flat voice.

It chilled me. It was a genuine question. She didn't know — stranger in a strange land. How could this be? There was supposed to have been a battle, a grand battle to fight against this. But there hadn't been, just quietly, the most horrific had happened. "Am I supposed to answer that? You steal my girlfriend's body, and you want my help."

"I didn't steal," again, no emotion.

"She gave it to you freely?"

She looked around as though puzzled and moved a few steps. "There's pain here," she murmured.

I looked at her with confusion, unsure what she was referring to. "You mean in being alive?" I asked. Now my voice was shaking with rage.

She slowly stretched out her arm and brought her hand closer to her face. "In this body, it hurts to be in this body."

"It was made for someone else," I answered slowly, trying to quell my desire to lash out at this thing.

"Do you have pain? Being in that body?"

I shook my head, "Don't you remember what it's like to be alive? There's always pain."

It was Annie's eyes but confused and bewildered. "I don't remember."

"You don't belong here now." My voice was trembling. I wanted to shake her, shake her violently, until she just left.

"This body was made for me," she rambled.

"No," I rasped. "This body was fashioned for someone else's soul, not yours. You can't have peace trying to take what belongs to another." I stared at her, feeling complete anguish, feeling a thousand different things. "If you try, it will tear you apart."

She looked at me blankly. She wasn't getting it.

110

"Take her back," the voice whispered in my mind.

I understood clearly. Someone had put the vision in my head. "I need to take you somewhere," I said, simply following the guidance I desperately needed.

Sometimes when I look back and remember what happened that first month in summer so long ago, I think perhaps it was a product of my fevered writer's imagination. I find it difficult to fully accept what I lived through. And I am more than sure that if I related the tale as fact rather than fiction, the world would sneer at me and consider it some sort of publicity ploy to attract attention. But in quiet moments, I can only say that you should consider the fact that there is so much more around you than the world your eyes see. What you see barely scratches the surface.

Dusk was descending as Lucy Bonner, for I had fully embraced the recognition that she now inhabited Annie's body, and I rode down a lonely road to the disintegrating remnants of the White Marsh church.

She didn't talk much. Oddly, it seemed as though the transition had sapped a good measure of her confidence which was just as well. The last thing I wanted was more inappropriate offers, and at this point, I didn't trust myself to repress my rage.

"My vision is not well," she spoke.

I didn't answer, just turned into the deserted shell driveway of the old church. I grabbed a flashlight from the glove compartment, realizing we would soon be in darkness. As I reached for it, I brushed against her knee briefly, and even that slight contact made me recoil inside. It was unbelievable how passionately I had made love to that same body hours ago and now. Now the thought of touching her disgusted me profoundly. It wasn't Annie. It wasn't Annie's beautiful soul. It was something that felt it was her right to take her away from me. And part of me, well, yes, most of me, hated her for it.

I got out of the car and waited for her to follow. Her movements were awkward. It was clear that she was having trouble maneuvering in the stolen skin.

Then she moved beside me, eyes on the deteriorating structure before her. "What is this place? I do not know it."

"It's a church built where Reverend Elstrott's church used to be."

There was a marked hesitation. "I fear that place."

I laughed sharply, crushed by the irony. "This is the world you so desperately wanted to be a part of Lucy Bonner. It is filled with fear." I began to walk forward to the gaping hole that used to be its entrance, and I heard Lucy Bonner shuffling behind me. I wondered if I was being too hard on her. But I wanted to show her the harshness of what she was choosing.

"Teach her," the voice whispered, concurring with my instincts.

I walked into the darkness of the building, feeling Lucy behind me. The flashlight illuminated only patches of the room as I shone it — the pulpit, the pews. "It is cold here," she spoke into the darkness.

It wasn't really. It was muggy from the summer heat that had beat down on the walls of the building all day, but evidently, she felt the coldness.

I could feel it expanding. It had begun as we were driving in the car, the awareness, almost as if someone was pressing on it, the middle of my forehead. And knowledge, knowledge I now remembered from those in the forest came to me.

"You're cold because the body is dying."

"What?" she said with evident terror. I shone the flashlight across her face so that I could see it. There was fear. There was fear all over her.

I spoke again with knowledge that did not belong to me. "It was not created for you, this shell. It will not sustain for you. You cannot take what is not yours."

"I want to live again," she rasped angrily.

"This is not your life to live. This life was created for this soul to learn. This spirit that you once shared chose to learn through this soul. Your place is somewhere else. There is other life for you, but not here."

"I have waited. It is mine to take," she spoke angrily, like a child having a tantrum.

"What you take will be dust to you. What you steal will be pain for you. You cannot step out of the natural order of existence." My voice, but another's knowledge, spoke through me with confidence.

She was crying, sobbing, and I could feel the confusion and the horror. And near, so close, I could feel the door opening and the voices calling to her, comforting — her parents, her sisters, and brothers calling to her.

"I fear."

"Fear is where you are now. Pain is where you are now," my voice and another's thoughts. "You must choose Lucy Bonner. You must choose."

She fell to her knees, shivering in wracking sobs, tormented sobs that washed over my skin, such despair. But I waited, knowing what was happening. I could feel her soul separating from the body, painfully wrenching away, then moving toward that door that had opened. Something shifted in me as I felt Lucy Bonner leave this world, as though a knife that had been in my gut all my life was finally pulled out. It still hurt, but now, just now, there was a possibility that it could heal.

113

Epilogue

I didn't remain in Kilmarnock for more than one more week. When Annie returned to consciousness, she was disoriented and completely drained of energy. I took her home, and she slept for the entire next day, and when she awoke, she was subdued, not really wanting to discuss much about what had happened. Distant, yes, but I stayed with her through her aunt's funeral. And before I left, it seemed as though Flora Catlett was on her way to a full recovery.

Bess Greenlief seemed amiable to breaking my lease. In a way, it seemed as though the whole town was walking around in a bit of a haze, not understanding exactly why. But we understood. I asked Annie to come home with me, but she said she needed time. She would be visiting her parents for a while up North before she made her move. All her ties to Kilmarnock had been severed.

I play with the idea from time to time of writing a novel about Lucy Bonner, but in some way, it feels like a desecration to me. I've come to accept that it was my own karma that brought me to that small town in Virginia that summer. My own karma that I hope in some way I've discharged. And often, my heart still aches when I remember. But now, there is a difference. I have something that I feel I have been lacking my whole life. I have hope.

Finis

The House at Pritchard Place
A New Orleans Paranormal Mystery (#3)
6 x 9 Softcover 136 pages
ISBN 978-1613422922

Nothing is really wrong with the old Warrick House on Dante St., except that there most certainly is. Nothing is exactly wrong with its new mysterious owner except that Elise is sure something doesn't add up. It isn't obvious, but sometimes the most dangerous things aren't. In the third installment of The New Orleans Paranormal Mystery series, with the help of her very psychic sister and her children, the Breslin clan, Elise Ashford is about to embark on a wild rescue mission straight into another dimension that will land her squarely somewhere she doesn't expect, right back into her past. She'll land full circle; in a childhood home whose memory still haunts her to this day — The House at Pritchard Place.

A Quiet Moment
6 x 9 Softcover 295 pages
ISBN 978-1-61342-326-4

Jacob Wyss is caught in a rut, in fact, on the verge of being engulfed by it. After an excruciating and disillusioning divorce, his life as an artist in a sleepy-college town at the foot of the Appalachian mountains has become quiet, routine, and maddening in its predictability. One wintry day, his deep restlessness drives him out in precarious conditions to a largely empty bookstore nearly devoid of another living soul, nearly.

Aimee Marston isn't like everyone else. On the surface, she lives a sedate life working as a feature writer for a small local newspaper in addition to several other editorial jobs to help make ends meet. But just beneath, her existence is largely not her own. She is a sensitive, an empathic psychic, guided by her calling to use her gifts to help others. Unfortunately, as a result, her secretiveness has made her defensive and protective of herself, preventing her from having much of a life.

A psychic call for help sends Aimee out on a freezing January morning, where her destiny and Jacob's collide, spiraling both their lives onto an unexpected and often disturbing track. Two lonely souls connect, not by accident, but by design. Theirs is the intersection of two spiritual paths, two lovers who must struggle to overcome the phantoms of a past life, as well as the challenges of their own inner demons to carve out an extraordinary future together.

Treading on Borrowed Time
6 x 9 Softcover 198 pages
ISBN 978-1-61342-214-4

For Julia Moreau, life seems complicated. Emerging from a failed marriage and managing a lifetime of diabetes, she lives alone in her childhood home, where she communicates with the spirit of her Great Aunt Lilia. But Julia doesn't have a clue what complicated is until she is thrust into being the key chess piece in a match between two powerful men of extraordinary abilities on the wild hunt for a mystical creature hidden in the heart of New Orleans' French Quarter. Will Julia lose her soul to the karma of a devastating past life or her heart to the love of a man driven by dark forces? What is clear is that whichever way she turns, she is *Treading on Borrowed Time*.

Sanctuary of Echoes
6 x 9 Softcover 338 pages
ISBN 978-1-61342-211-3

Ghosts unacknowledged do not sleep.

Corey Knight has resigned herself to a quiet, reclusive life spent living out the rest of her days in her childhood home on the fringes of New Orleans' French Quarter. But the unexpected specter of her deceased father plunges her into a mad quest for a missing supernatural weapon unearthed long ago. And unfortunately, her only ally is a lost love she once betrayed.

Iain Shaw returns to New Orleans, a city he abandoned a decade before while fleeing a devastating past. Here, he is forced to confront it again in the visage of the woman he once adored - one that he is now determined to get back at any cost.

Follow them both in a wild paranormal tale of discovery and redemption as they confront and unearth the echoes of a buried and unyielding truth that once tore them irreparably apart.

Dragonflies - Journeys into the Paranormal
6 x 9 Softcover 120 pages
ISBN 978-1-88756-072-6

A powerful wizard, love-crossed ghosts, a mysterious dark warrior, and an enigmatic time traveler -- a mystical wordsmith entices you into the world of the paranormal with a collection of inspired stories. Each tale takes the journey of the dragonfly imbued with the momentum and energy of change, following a winding path that will ultimately lead you to find the truth buried beneath perception.

A Ghost of a Chance
6 x 9 Softcover 174 pages
ISBN 978-1-88756-050-4

Jack Brennan, an ambitious high-powered attorney, dies, only to find himself constrained to a peculiar afterlife as an earth-bound spirit trapped in an old Virginia farmhouse with a very much living, reclusive writer of campy vampire novels. Hallie Barkly recovering from a painful and disillusioning divorce, has forged a career and exorcised her demons by writing under the pseudonym of Sebastian Winters. Their lives intersect, and two unconventional lovers are brought together under insurmountable circumstances. Together they must battle an unseen force hell-bent on possessing Hallie's life and bridge death itself to make possible what cannot be - to find a chance.

Breaking Through the Pale
6 x 9 Softcover 92 pages
ISBN 978-1-88756-045-0

Journey with metaphysical author Evelyn Klebert into a collection of short stories that travel beyond the pale into the unpredictable realm of the paranormal.
In "A Grey Mourning," a disillusioned man encounters a mysterious being on the foggy streets of New Orleans. "Contact" is a tale of automatic writing, when a young artist establishes communication with a spirit guide, and the victim of a car crash unravels the true nature of her existence in "Dancing on the Threshold." The final tale is called "Isolation," in which a confused and disoriented woman finds herself in an old, quaint house where she

must piece together the mystical implications *surrounding her predicament.*

Explanations
6 x 9 Softcover 82 pages
ISBN 978-1-93493-515-6

In this, her second poetry collection, Evelyn Klebert takes us down the intricate path of a personal journey. Life, with its particular struggles, pitfalls, and ultimately triumphs, clearly begins to mirror a universal path, the quest for answers that we all ultimately pursue. In this reflective, esoteric collection, we can all explore and seek some of life's elemental mysteries and, hopefully, when all is said and done, emerge with some *Explanations.*

The Witches' Own
6 x 9 Softcover 124 pages
ISBN 978-1-61342-058-4

On the surface, things seem quiet and serene in the picturesque coastal village of Kilmarnock, Virginia. But something unseen roams its lush forests as the past and present collide, and the unthinkable begins to wreak its vengeance. Young Lucy Bonner is executed for witchcraft in the town's distant and brutal past. Her death triggers an unholy chain of events that grasp at the restless heart of novelist Peter McQuade, spurring him towards a quest to uncover the dark and terrifying truth.

The Left Palm
And Other Halloween Tales of the Supernatural
6 x 9 Softcover 104 pages
ISBN 978-1-93493-556-9

Halloween is the time of year when that veil between worlds is thinned, and you can just catch a quick glimpse into the realm of the unknowable. In this collection of short stories, Evelyn Klebert takes you to a place where ordinary life splinters into the sphere of the paranormal.

The journey begins with one woman's unstoppable quest for vengeance against a supernatural creature in "Wolves" and continues in an old historical graveyard where a horrifying discovery is uncovered in "Emma Fallon." In "The Soul Shredder," a psychiatrist's unusual patient opens his eyes to a disturbing new view of reality, while in "Wildflowers," a woman strikes up a supernatural friendship with impossible implications. And in "The Left Palm," a fortuneteller in the French Quarter receives a most unexpected and terrifying customer.

White Harbor Road
And Other Tales of Paranormal Romance
6 x 9 Softcover 130 pages
ISBN 978-1-61342-066-9

A psychic soul mate, a time traveler, a horror writer, and an enigmatic stranger take a selection of resilient, life-battered heroines to a place of paranormal healing and transformation. In this collection of short stories, White Harbor Road is the last stop where life's burdens and hardships evolve into something unexpected.

The Broken Vow
Vol. I of The Clandestine Exploits of a Werewolf
6 x 9 Softcover 140 pages
ISBN 978-1-61342-133-8

In the heart of every man, there is a history. In the heart of every monster, there is a story. In this first installment of *The Clandestine Exploits of a Werewolf*, Ethan Garraint is on a vendetta that begins in the heart of the Pyrenees with the fall of Montségur and leads him to the streets of New Orleans nearly five hundred years later. But the person he chases isn't really a man anymore, and Ethan has been a werewolf for almost a millennium. With the aid of a gifted seer, he is on a blood hunt that will culminate in a journey that crosses the line between heaven and earth and ends somewhere in between.

Travels into the Breach: Accounts of a Reclusive Mystic
6 x 9 Softcover 176 pages
ISBN 978-1-61342-323-3

At first glance, his life seems quiet, serene, and even uneventful. Malachi McKellan, a 65 five-year-old widower and author of esoteric books, lives largely as a recluse in a house situated just off the banks of Bayou St. John in New Orleans. But unbeknownst to most, he is also a bit of a detective, a specific kind of detective whose specialty is psychic attacks. Alongside his lifelong companion and spirit guide Simon Tull, a nineteenth century, twenty something English gent, Malachi battles the unseen, and is an unacknowledged hero to the most vulnerable - most of the population who have no idea what is really happening beneath the surface of the world in which they live.

In this collection of adventures, Malachi McKellan and Simon Tull wage war against the most insidious elements of the paranormal. In "The Three," Malachi and Simon come to the aid of a young woman being victimized by a group of dark witches. An old apartment building is the scene of an unimaginable battle against monstrous forces in "The Lost Soul." Malachi and Simon find themselves strategizing against a psychic vampire in "Obsession," and "The Hotel" turns back time to the 1980s where Malachi confronts a demonic spirit. In "Between," a past life is revisited as Malachi attempts to rescue a beloved sister from committing her existence to vengeance, and "The

Wedding" takes a personal turn when Malachi must confront painful truths while endeavoring to protect his niece from a potentially devastating union. Travel into the Breach with a pair of paranormal warriors who choose to confront overwhelming forces on a battlefield unsuspected by most.

Considerations
6 x 9 Softcover 68 pages
ISBN 978-1-88756-062-7

Sometimes the struggle to understand the meaning and complexities of living comes down to a single moment of introspection or a fleeting yet meaningful reflection. This collection of poetry by Evelyn Klebert takes you down a winding path of self-discovery where the resolution may not always be absolute, but the journey is indeed unforgettable. It is a wide and varied map of inspired poetry for your examination and consideration.

Appointment with the Unknown: The Hotel Stories
6 x 9 Softcover 151 pages
ISBN 978-1613423608

A hotel, for most, represents a normal place, a predictable realm of commonality. One might even go as far to say a safe space, the reliable where nothing particularly unusual is expected to happen. Or is it? Dimensional traveling, spirit guides, mystical storms, and soul mates separated by time are only a few elements dotting this supernatural landscape. Drop into a collection of romantic paranormal stories where that place of commonality is only the threshold, the jumping-off point, for extraordinary adventures into the unknown.

The Tethering: A Portent of Crows
6 x 9 Softcover 201 pages
ISBN 978-1613425992

Deborah Brandt's beloved Aunt Gena always told her that she was special, a bit different, and would have to live her life, unlike other people. Of course, this she disregarded as the ramblings of her lovely but notably eccentric aunt. Although there were the things that Aunt Gena said that seemed true — like Deborah being sensitive to energy shifts, having potentially psychic impressions, and dreaming of a spirit guide — none of it could be real. But the most ridiculous thing that her Aunt Gena told her before she died was that someone special was out there for her. She said that he was an extraordinary man who was not only her perfect match but someone who she would learn from so that they could help the world in difficult times. How ridiculous! It sounds like a fairy tale, and no such person exists.

Daniel Wren is unique. He has been raised and trained from a young age to hone his psychic gifts. He lives in a world unimagined by most. And he has been waiting for years to contact his counterpart, soulmate, if you will. But the problem is that she is painfully unaware of the type of life that he lives and the life she would be entering into if they came together.

His dilemma becomes how best to proceed. How can he win her over and move forward before outside forces take that decision away from him?

The Lady in the Blue Dress
6 x 9 Softcover 214 pages
ISBN 978-1613426005

When she was a child, Mika Devalieur was introduced to her grandmother's most precious possession — a priceless and mysterious painting that she simply called The Lady in the Blue Dress. Upon Adele St. Clair's death, the painting is left in the care of her granddaughter with only one stipulation. Mika must hand over the family heirloom to a total stranger. Mika Devalieur desperately wants to deny her beloved grandmother's last request, but she can't. Torn between her Gran's last wishes and her desire to hold onto the Lady, she ultimately journeys to rural Virginia, where an enigmatic man shows her that this painting is only the beginning.

What quickly becomes clear is that James Clairmont knows much more about her and the Lady than he is letting on. He begins to slowly unravel a powerful supernatural connection that spans three generations of her family. Mika finds herself desperate to uncover the entire truth before she falls in love with a man filled with so many secrets — secrets about him, about her, and most especially about The Lady in the Blue Dress. (First published on Kindle Vella, episodes 1-23.)

Visit Evelyn's website at:
www.evelynklebert.com

Cornerstone Book Publishers
www.cornerstonepublishers.com